Without warn ... **space and tilte** ... **the shoulders** ... **into his smiling** ... **rushed to her head. Before she could chastise him, he brought her upright.**

She hated surprises. Being out of control ranked number one on her never-to-do list. Dante threatened all of that. From the few stories Vanessa had told her about him, they were as different as a waltz and a tango. "Talk."

Should she be feeling the deep rumble of his laughter against her chest? When had he pulled her so close? She tried to create space between them. His hand splayed at her back made it impossible.

"Do you ever loosen up?"

She snapped her head up. Even though she was wearing stilettos, he loomed over her. "You've met me, what? All of twice? You have no idea who I am."

He leaned in close, his breath tickling her ear as he whispered, "But I'd like to."

All thoughts of why she'd come on the dance floor escaped as he pressed his cheek against hers. For once in her life Lanelle lost herself in the gentle sway of a man's embrace.

Dear Reader,

Lanelle Murphy's life hasn't been easy. Wealth and success have helped to cushion the blows thrown her way, but tragedy is hard to endure no matter who you are. Lanelle has closed herself off from men, and so Dante Sanderson has no chance with her when they meet. Dante isn't without his issues when it comes to previous relationships, either, but he's willing to try.

Dante realizes if he doesn't do something drastic, he'll never have Lanelle. He devises a trip to the most romantic country in the world—Dante's words—to help her overcome whatever prevents her from pursuing a romantic relationship. When Dante discovers Lanelle's secret, the doubts settle in.

I hope you enjoy the emotional drama, laughter, romance and trip to Italy.

Nana Prah

A Perfect Caress

NANA PRAH

HARLEQUIN® KIMANI™ ROMANCE

Recycling programs
for this product may
not exist in your area.

ISBN-13: 978-0-373-86480-5

A Perfect Caress

HARLEQUIN®
www.Harlequin.com

Printed in U.S.A.

Nana Prah first discovered romance in a book from her eighth-grade summer reading list and has been obsessed with it ever since. Her fascination with love inspired her to write in her favorite genre, where happily-ever-after is the rule.

She is a published author of contemporary, multicultural romances. Her books are sweet with a touch of spice. When she's not writing, she's overindulging in chocolate, enjoying life with friends and family and tormenting nursing students into being the best nurses the world has ever seen.

Books by Nana Prah

Harlequin Kimani Romance

A Perfect Caress

To my greatest role model, my late mother, Theresa Prah.

Acknowledgments

To the women who hung out with me
when they didn't have to. Thanks for helping to mold me
into who I am today. I will always love and cherish you.
Aunt Waynet, Aunt Frances, Aunt Sherry,
Aunt Elizabeth P., Aunty Tej, Aunt Betsy, Aunt Lucy,
Lisa S., Sister (former) Elizabeth, Marianne S.

A huge thanks to my inner circle who have supported
me in my writing and allowed me to harass them with
questions and beta reads. Cathrina Constantine,
Debbie Christiana, Kiru Taye, Empi Baryeh
and Ortanyi Arrington, you are all the best.

I'm throwing an avalanche of gratitude at Rachel Burkot
for grabbing me and tossing me into the Kimani family,
and at Carly Silver for securing my place.

Thank you, Toshia T., for helping to promote my work.
Toshia, this is for you.

Chapter 1

Tackling a person to the ground in order grab the last piece of cake would be wrong. Lanelle Murphy had trouble convincing herself of this little truth. Maybe not so much wrong as bad and kind of depressing. Unless it ended up being the best cake ever baked.

Her gaze never wandered from the prize while a suspected perpetrator remained in the periphery. At five feet eight inches, Lanelle increased her already long stride to eat up more of the ground at a faster rate.

Their hands landed on the clear plastic container holding the triple-layered moist chocolate cake covered with scrumptious, rich chocolate icing at the same time.

Since Lanelle's palm touched the container with his warm fingers wrapped around hers, it meant she'd gotten to it first. The cake belonged to her. The stranger's resigning breath pushed away any idea she may have had of elbowing him in the ribs before running toward the cashier and dropping money on the counter without stopping.

Lanelle tilted her head to the man without deigning to look at him. If she gave him her full attention, she'd do the kind thing and relinquish the treat. After receiving a disappointing update about a project close to her heart, she deserved it.

After almost two years of planning and fund-raising to build a new neonatal unit in the hospital, Lanelle felt like giving up. Dealing with the other members of the hospital board had proved tedious.

The problems creeping up with the construction set their timeline back and deepened the financial ditch. The funds they'd raised had run out faster than expected, and she couldn't understand how it had happened. They'd been meticulous in their calculations. After going through the books with her personal accountant this past week, they'd found nothing amiss.

Maybe she should've accepted her father's help when he'd offered it, but she figured it couldn't be difficult to construct a hospital wing. It wasn't like they were building a whole hospital from the ground up. It turned out that more went into it than she'd researched.

Lanelle had been trained by the best to ensure things happened the way they should, but this project was draining the life out of her.

She needed this cake. "Hi," she said instead of telling him to get his paw off her pastry.

"Hello. It looks like we both want the same piece of cake."

The deep rumble of his voice enticed her but wouldn't detract her. "Looks that way." Didn't this man know not to get between a woman and her chocolate? She turned her head to get a good look at the enemy. They stood so close she had to angle her head back in order to see his face.

Great. The guy who threatened her sanity turned out to be at least six-two. She could've picked a better day to wear her cutest pair of Tabitha Simmons ballerina flats.

More than his height caused her breath to hitch. His

sienna-brown eyes, contrasting with skin almost as rich and dark as the cake, made for a gorgeous man.

"Would you be interested in the vanilla, by any chance?" His grin drew her attention to full lips covering a set of even white teeth, adding to the squishy feeling in her stomach.

"As tempting as it looks with those rainbow sprinkles, I'd prefer the chocolate." She'd finished playing nice with the handsome stranger sporting the cutest little afro she'd seen in a while and pulled the cake toward her. "Since my hand is on the container, it means I reached it first, so *technically* it's mine."

"On a normal day I'd agree, but I need this cake."

She snorted. "Let me guess. You have PMS and you're about to take down anyone who gets in the way of getting your fix." Her frown melded into a grin at his burst of laughter.

"No. My niece is about to find out if she's still in remission from the cancer she beat last year. She asked me last night to pick her up a piece of chocolate cake from *this* cafeteria when I came to join the meeting after her MRI. She insisted no other would do."

Lanelle squinted in an attempt to assess if he'd given her a line. Detecting no guile in his expression, she released the box. He didn't let go of her hand.

Sliding her fingers out of his grasp, she crossed her arms over her chest. "I hope your niece is healthy."

"Thank you. I know she'll appreciate that I almost got beaten up for her cake." He held out his right hand. "I'm Dante Sanderson."

"I wouldn't have fought you. Maybe just taken you down," she mumbled as she placed her hand in his. She pulled it away at the bizarre sensation of tingles racing up her arm to her scalp.

She tucked her hand behind her, confused at her body's reaction.

He raised an eyebrow. "You think it's a possibility?"

"A fact."

"Hmm. You sound sure of yourself."

A slight dip of her head to the side would have to suffice for an answer as they walked to the front of the cafeteria.

He placed the single item on the counter and waited to be checked out. Before she had the chance to move past him, he asked, "What's your name?"

She paused, wondering if she should answer with the truth. His charm had an uncomfortable effect on her. What did she have to lose? She'd never see him again. "Lanelle Murphy."

"Can I walk you to wherever you're going?"

She backed away as her gaze fell on the cake with regret. "It's better if you don't. I'd like your niece to be a happy girl. Take care." Before he could speak again, she blended into the throng of people passing by.

Dante dashed a ten-dollar bill onto the counter and rushed out of the cafeteria without waiting for his change. Lanelle had headed to the left, so he made his way down that hallway. It had been a while since a woman had fascinated him. His heart still raced.

For once his height wasn't an advantage when it came to finding someone in a crowd. A tall, medium brown–skinned woman with her hair piled in a tight bun turned out to be more difficult to find during lunchtime near a cafeteria than he'd anticipated. She'd vanished.

He relaxed his outstretched neck. The news he'd received in the morning, about his company winning the bid to install the flooring and countertops for the new hospital wing, had brought him to the hospital early to sign the contract. It would pull his business in a whole new direction. One that would leave the company free and clear in his name. Winning him full ownership of the company.

If only they'd get good news from his niece's doctor, he could have a celebration.

The vibration of his phone diverted his attention from the now-waning search for the mystery woman. The screen lit up with a picture of Vanessa's bright, smiling face. A year ago his knees had buckled when they'd found out her Hodgkin's lymphoma had been kicked to the curb. If only it would stay there.

He answered the phone with "I've got the cake, CocoVan." The girl loved chocolate. Everyone swore that her first word had been "cocoa," as she'd reached for the candy bar her mother had been eating.

Vanessa giggled instead of chastising him for using the nickname she claimed to loathe. "More great news."

"More?"

"Where are you?" She evaded his question.

Dante continued to scan the hall for the elusive Lanelle. *Give it up. She's long gone.* "Near the cafeteria you strong-armed me into going to."

"You offered, Uncle D. Mom wants you to meet us in the parking garage."

"What about the results?"

Did she just emit laughter of hysteria or of joy? His palms sweated as he turned on his heel in haste toward the opposite direction from the one the mystery lady had taken. Had they gotten the news already? Was it bad? No, he wouldn't allow his mind to go there. "Are you okay?" *Please say yes.*

"Just meet us. Mom's getting all clingy again." She hung up, sending him flying through the hospital corridors in an attempt to reach his niece without having a heart attack from the fear ready to choke him.

When he arrived, from halfway across the parking lot, one thing hit Dante: huge smiles erupted from each of their faces.

When his niece noticed him, she ran over and grabbed the chocolate cake from his hands. "You're the best."

"What's going on?"

The fingers his older sister, Cynthia, held over her lips couldn't hide the ear-to-ear grin. "Vanessa's still in remission."

Dante froze. His gaze roamed over to his brother-in-law, whose head bobbed up and down so fiercely, Dante feared damage to his spine. When he looked at his niece, his dazed state broke. Lifting her, he spun so her legs arced behind her.

Vanessa's laughter transformed into a groan. "I'm dizzy."

So was he, but he didn't care. Setting her down, he ensured she didn't fall after she stumbled. "This is amazing." He'd become a proud member of the irrepressible smile club.

Cynthia and her husband joined them in a huddled hug. Their prayers of gratitude weren't loud, yet he knew they could be heard in the loftiest of places.

Breaking away, Dante didn't care that they saw him wiping away tears. With a sniffle he asked, "How come you found out without me?"

"We wanted to wait, but Little Miss Hot-Pants here—" Cynthia pointed to her only daughter "—begged us to go in early when the receptionist announced we could see the doctor."

Alan's laughter echoed through the parking lot. "That's not how I recall it." Cynthia's husband was one of the only men he knew who had the ability to call his sister out when she implemented her overbearing ways. "Switch the names and you have a truer account."

Vanessa sidled up to her father and swung an arm around his waist. "I wanted to wait for you, but Mom didn't even ask me when she snatched my arm and dragged me into the office."

Cynthia dismissed the duo with a flick of her hand. "It's all good. My baby girl is healthy. Nothing else matters."

"Amen." Alan raised a hand in response.

Dante became aware of his surroundings. "What are we doing out here? Let's pick Ryan up and party.

How does McKnight's sound?"

"Delicious." Cynthia smacked her lips. "I could use some soul food I didn't cook myself."

Clasping his palms, Dante set the plan in motion. "Great. How about you and Alan get the hyperactive child and meet us there? Vanessa can drive my car."

Vanessa's emitted screeches had Dante concerned for his eardrums. "You're going to let me drive your Lamborghini? Really?"

For once, he'd relinquish control of his beloved custom-tailored car. "Today is the day to rejoice, and you mean more to me than the car ever will. Since you've been hounding me about it since I bought it two years ago, I figure today is as good a day as any."

Vanessa's giddiness as she tackled him in a hug solidified Dante's decision, making his heart swell even further.

Alan nodded. "Sounds like a plan."

Cynthia extended her arms to her daughter, and Vanessa stepped into them without question.

Dante watched the touching scene. The family had been through hell and back since Vanessa had been diagnosed. Now life would go back to as normal as it could be, with the threat of cancer always hanging over them.

Vanessa broke the embrace and walked to Dante with her cake in one hand and the other palm up with her fingers wiggling. "The keys."

He fished the keys out of his pocket and handed them to his niece with one warning. "Be careful."

"Of course I will, Uncle D," she said as she waved her dessert parcel. "I didn't make it this far to let it all go for some speed."

The cake brought to mind the mystery woman he'd met in the cafeteria. Other than announcing he'd lost a beautiful Nubian princess over the hospital speakers and saying she should hightail it back to the cafeteria, there was nothing he could do to find her. Shaking his head at the regret of having to wait to start his search for her, he hooked an arm around his niece's shoulders and led her to his car.

Chapter 2

The sudden scream put Lanelle on full alert. Taking in her surroundings, she wished she'd had her driver drop her off at the meeting instead of insisting on driving herself.

Four rows across the barrier where she'd parked, an older and a younger woman hugged. Lanelle spied on the pair, wondering what had happened to make them embrace in the middle of a parking garage.

Considering the lot belonged to a hospital, morose thoughts of death and illness came to mind. Perhaps one was comforting the other.

Slipping herself out of the imaginary world she'd created for the people she'd never meet, Lanelle opened her door and slid behind the wheel of her favorite, yet least ostentatious, car. She sparked the engine of the navy blue Volvo S80. With the press of a button, the seat's massaging system eased the tension from her lower back.

After a few moments of bliss, she pulled out of her parking space. As she rounded the corner where the women had embraced, she noticed a tall, dark-skinned man standing in the middle of the aisle. How could this be when she'd done such a good job escaping him earlier? Distracted, she slammed on the brake.

Realizing too late she'd drawn their attention, Lanelle pressed the gas in an attempt to ease past without being seen. Although the side windows were tinted, anyone outside the car had full view of her through the windshield.

Fate. Kismet. Destiny. All words of impossibility Lanelle didn't believe in shuffled themselves around in her head. What had been the chances of ever seeing Dante again when she'd given him her name? Obviously, the odds had been pretty darn good.

The attempt to make herself invisible by scrunching low in her seat failed. He disturbed her in a warm-feeling-at-her-center kind of way. The last thing she needed in her life was to be attracted to someone.

Lanelle knew the moment the cake stealer recognized her. Waving her down, he stepped over to her window. For a split second she thought of zooming past so she'd never have to listen to the deep timbre of his voice again. *Isn't that what I thought when I left him in the cafeteria?*

From the impression she'd gotten of him earlier, Lanelle figured Dante was the kind of man a woman could have fun with but never tie down. She wasn't in the market for either.

His broad grin sent a flutter skidding through her belly. "Hi. Funny meeting you here."

Uncanny, but stranger things had happened. She'd have been out of the parking lot a good five minutes ago if she hadn't forgotten her briefcase in the boardroom in her dash out of an adjourned meeting for chocolate cake therapy. "If you find it even mildly amusing, then you have a weird sense of humor."

"I've been accused of it a time or two."

She smirked.

"You have a pretty smile."

Yes, the man's a charmer. She straightened in her seat, thinking she might feel more comfortable if he didn't tower over her. *Whom am I kidding? The man's a giant.* He'd dwarf her even if she was standing in three-inch heels. "Thank you." Keeping things light and polite would be the easiest way out without hurting his ego. "Nice seeing you again. Take care."

"Wait." He motioned to the young woman she'd seen hugging the older one. "Vanessa, come here."

Lanelle's mouth watered as the girl brought her chocolate cake closer. Good to know he hadn't been lying.

"Vanessa, meet Lanelle. The woman I almost got into a fight with to make sure you got your cake."

Lanelle put the car in Park and eased her foot off the brake. Reaching out the window, she extended her right hand to the young woman. The dimple she displayed in each cheek brought out Lanelle's own smile. Her test results must've been good. "Nice to meet you, Vanessa."

"You, too." Vanessa gave Dante her attention. "What do you mean about the cake?"

Dante's light brown eyes gleamed as he focused on Lanelle while answering his niece. "This gorgeous woman was on the cusp of initiating a takedown over the last piece of chocolate cake in the cafeteria."

Lanelle's face flamed as Vanessa turned to her with an openmouthed stare. "You've tried the cake," Lanelle defended. "Tell me what you would've done."

Vanessa nodded. "Snatched it and run."

Lanelle liked Vanessa's honesty. "Exactly."

"But you decided to give it up." Vanessa drew her eyebrows together. "Why?"

"Your uncle told me you'd be getting news today."

Vanessa placed a hand on her chest. "You gave up the best chocolate cake in the world for me? That's so nice of you." Then she looked down at the container and pushed it through the open window. "You can have it." Hopping from foot to foot, she burst out with "I'm in remission."

Joy beyond anything Lanelle had ever experienced for a stranger overwhelmed her. Shoving the cake back at Vanessa, she opened her door and hugged the girl. "How wonderful. I'm so happy for you."

Vanessa held her tight, their upper bodies swaying from side to side as they giggled. When they separated, the reality of what Lanelle, oftentimes accused of being conservative to a fault, had just done hit her.

Three pairs of eyes stared at them as she stepped away and attempted to regain her composure.

An older version of Vanessa moved to the young woman's side. "Who's this?" The question was made less severe by the crinkles at the corners of her eyes as she grinned.

"Lanelle," Vanessa answered. "She gave up this cake for me without fighting Uncle D."

Cynthia held out her hand. "Nice to meet you, Lanelle. I'm Cynthia. I'm not sure what's going on with the cake, but thank you for not hurting my brother."

The woman's grip was firm as they shook. "It's not like it sounds."

"Yes, it is," Dante gloated.

Lanelle hurled Dante a look that should've had him quivering. He threw her off-kilter by laughing. "No, it isn't," Lanelle protested. "I'm happy Vanessa is cancer free. I guess I got a little overwhelmed." It took a split second for her to decide to share her own news. "My mother is a breast cancer survivor, so I understand just how good it is to get such wonderful news."

"I'm happy for you and your mother." Cynthia held an arm out to the man on her right. "This is my husband, Alan."

The last set of handshakes took place, and then Lanelle said, "I should be going. Congratulations, Vanessa." She gripped the handle of her car to open it.

Vanessa touched her arm. "We're going out to celebrate. Would you like to come with us?"

Lanelle looked at the girl, then glanced at Dante, who seemed just as surprised by his niece's offer. She would've expected that from him. "I think this might be a family celebration."

She was a reserved person by nature; it didn't help that Lanelle's conservative childhood hadn't allowed her to open up to too many people out of fear of them finding out she was an heiress and attempting to manipulate her for their own benefit. It had only taken a couple negative experiences to know that her life was smoother when she kept to herself.

Cynthia looked at the trio. "Do you all know each other?"

"I met Lanelle in the cafeteria about fifteen minutes ago," Dante said.

Vanessa looked at her mother. "Uncle D introduced us just now. But she seems so cool." She turned to Lanelle. "I'd really like it if you joined us," Vanessa insisted.

Dante licked his lips before adding, "Me, too."

She had to stay away from such a dangerous man, even though an unexpected urge propelled her to spend time with this family. "I have something to take care of at home."

Cynthia grabbed her daughter by the arm. "It was nice meeting you, Lanelle."

Alan waved as they dragged Vanessa away. She broke free of her mother's grip and came back. "Can I have your number?"

She had no idea what propelled her, but Lanelle found herself rattling off the digits to the bubbly young lady, whose presence alone made her feel lighter.

"I'll call you," Vanessa promised as she backed away

toward her parents, who stood in front of a sweet red Lamborghini.

Dante's presence dazed her as she tore her attention from the car to him. No man should be so handsome and have charm oozing from his pores to affect the innocent women of the world. Under the suave exterior lay, she sensed, someone who possessed a depth of character it would take the rest of her life to unearth. *Someone worth getting to know?* "I'd better go." Once again she reached for her door. Dante's hand stilled her. The warmth of his touch radiated up her arm, heating her in the most delicious way.

"Would you like to go out to dinner tomorrow night?"

She opened her mouth to speak and ended up drawing in a sharp breath when he stepped forward and crowded her. His spicy, citrusy scent enticed her. With a hard swallow, she stepped back, only to bump into her car. One way to get out of this. The destiny card.

Tilting her head up, she memorized his features, knowing she'd never see him again. "Let's do this. If we ever meet each other by accident again, I'll go out with you."

"You seem like a reasonable woman. What you just proposed isn't anywhere near rational. We've already met twice by chance. I think kismet has played its role."

Impressed, she tried to stay strong instead of falling into his invitation. "It's the way I live. Third time and you get a date." She pointed a French-tipped manicured finger at him. "By the way, I gave my number to Vanessa, not you. So don't even think about calling me. If fate wants us to go out, then we will."

He reached for her hand and held it between them, rubbing his thumb against her palm. The few seconds of sensual circles hardened her nipples. With reluctance, she pulled away.

He looked into her eyes. Not a hint of a smile appeared.

"I don't like this game, but we'll play it your way. Remember your promise, because we'll see each other again." He backed off.

The solidness of the car on her backside grounded her, helping her resist the desire to follow him as her body longed to do.

Tearing her gaze away, she turned her back on the temptation he presented and got into her car. With one last wave at Vanessa and her parents, she took off, refusing to acknowledge Dante with a goodbye.

No man would ever be able to provide her heart's desire, so why even bother with them at all?

Chapter 3

For once Dante was almost pleased to be chauffeured as his thoughts wandered back to the encounter with Lanelle in the parking garage. He relaxed as Vanessa navigated her way through the streets of Cleveland.

At a fresh red light Dante watched as she opened the lid on the dessert and scooped out a piece with a plastic fork. He should reprimand her for eating in his car, but fascination over what had brought him into contact with the most amazing woman he'd met in a long time took precedence.

Vanessa shook her head and slapped her leg. "Mmm, mmm, mmm. This is so good. Even better than I remember."

"I don't need to see it all in your mouth to know it's delicious. Let me try." Without any more coercion she placed a piece, albeit a small one compared with what she'd taken, onto the fork and slid it into his mouth. Not bad. Not worth a tussle, but he saw the appeal.

"What do you mean *not bad*? No wonder she turned you down for a date. If you can't appreciate fabulous cake, you probably can't appreciate her, either."

Did his niece just take a stranger's side over his? He couldn't blame her. Lanelle radiated something alluring beyond her obvious beauty. The memory of her flawless skin, large dark brown eyes, an adorable nose he could eat up and lips he had difficulty looking away from made him sigh.

Lanelle's poise and sophistication, along with her readiness to smile and celebrate life with a stranger, added to her charisma. He'd been inches from kissing her. Only the fact that his family stood so close watching their every move had stopped him. "Watch it. It's not too late to revoke your driving privileges on my car."

"You wouldn't. Not to someone who found out she's still free from cancer, now, would you?" Vanessa tried to pull off her sad, begging puppy-dog look but got diverted by the cake.

"We'll be eating soon."

"Mom's not here to threaten me, so I'm eating dessert first. Can we swing by the college? Art history is letting out now, and I want to show off a little to my friends."

Dante chuckled. "Fine, but don't expect me to get out of the car and wait on the corner while you do."

She shoved the half-empty container into his hands when the light turned green and the car behind them honked. "It'll only be for ten minutes."

"Either you showcase me and the car or there's no deal," Dante insisted.

"Okay."

He closed the lid on the cake after sneaking another forkful. "What made you get Lanelle's number?"

Vanessa flashed him a grin. "What made you ask her out?"

Smart-assed little girl. How Cynthia hadn't driven that annoying quality out of her by now was a mystery to everyone. He resorted to "I asked you first."

"I liked her. She seemed to be someone I could hang out with."

"Even though she's older?"

She shrugged. "*We* hang out."

"Because we're family."

Vanessa sucked her teeth as she made a left turn. "Uncle Xander is family, but I don't go places with him."

Dante held up a finger. "First of all, your dad's brother is nowhere near as cool as me, and second he lives in California, so you can't just pick up the phone and ask him to come get you. And don't you even mention my brother Emmanuel. With the number of kids he and his wife have, they can barely get out of the house."

"Whatever. My point is, age doesn't matter with friendship. Or did I hear it about love?"

"I concede."

Vanessa pulled the car over in front of a café a few blocks from her school, put it in Park and pressed the button to unlock the doors. "Please, Uncle D?"

He crossed his arms over his chest and looked out the windshield. One glance at her would break his resolve. There wasn't much he wouldn't do for his nieces and nephews, and they knew how to play him. "You can forget about me getting out of this car."

"How about if I talk you up to Lanelle when I call her?" The manipulative minx tapped a finger on the custom-designed steering wheel. "Maybe find out where she'll be, so you can bump into her."

Dante reached for the handle. "You can tell her how wonderful I am, but don't ask where she'll be at any point in time. The woman is not stupid." He opened the door. "You have twenty minutes. We still have to meet your parents and little brother at the restaurant. Your friends can sit in the car, but don't go joyriding."

He pulled out his phone. "I have an app that lets me see exactly where the car is at all times." She didn't need to know he had yet to learn how to use it.

"I promise. Thanks, Uncle D."

Curbside, he watched his precious niece and car roll down the street.

Vanessa's offer had been tempting, but he'd never get away with it if she became his informant. The two seemed to get along, but who knew if anything would come of their spark of friendship?

He had to find a way to see Lanelle again. Why would she deny the attraction blazing between them? *Maybe she's married.* A ring had adorned two fingers on her right hand, but the left hand was free. No matter the reason, he'd find her. He hadn't become successful in life by giving up, and he wouldn't do so with her.

On the other hand, if they were meant to be together, they'd meet again. He scoffed at the idea. *As long as my name is Dante Leroy Sanderson, I'll find her. Fate be damned.*

Toshia Covington panted hard as the StairMaster kicked her ass early the next morning.

Lanelle's own breath came out with less stress as she jogged at an easy pace on the treadmill next to her best friend. "Why don't you lower the intensity? I don't want to break out my CPR skills on you here in the gym."

Even sweating buckets, her best friend looked good. Toshia's thick hair swung in its ponytail as her hips swayed. Her large, dark brown, almond-shaped eyes remained bright even as sweat dripped into them. "What happened to *no pain, no gain*?"

"I think the person who coined the phrase died of a massive heart attack while not listening to his body."

Toshia let go of her machine's handle long enough to dab the sweat from her face with her towel. "Ha, ha, ha. How are things going with the NICU you're building?"

Lanelle puffed out a breath. "The wing is coming along

great in terms of construction, but we're running out of money." Saying the words out loud brought on a fresh wave of frustration.

"What?"

"Yeah, we have no idea what's going on. The books balance, but it doesn't make sense. The flooring and the fixtures are the only things remaining. And there's very little cash in the till."

Toshia stared at her. "How can that be?"

Thinking about it made her angrier with each minute. "You know how I was busy working on Dad's supersensitive project."

"You mean the one where I saw you once during the six-week period and you hardly slept?"

Lanelle shivered thinking about how much work had gone into the assignment. Every once in a while, when her father had a highly confidential financial project, he'd call her to head it. "Work on the NICU started at around the same time, but I couldn't say no to Dad."

"Plus, you're naive as hell and thought people would be honest."

"Who would try to extort money from a hospital trying to build a wing to help innocent babies?"

Toshia pursed her full, pinkish-brown lips to the side and tapped her chin in a pretense of thinking. "Let's see. Greedy-ass bastards with no concept of right or wrong come to mind."

"I'm not saying the money was stolen, but it wasn't well managed. We've gone through the books twice. The next step is to call a forensic accountant." She pushed an errant strand of hair behind her ear. "I feel like I'm on a crime show, only instead of dead bodies, it's all about paperwork."

Toshia shook her head. "None of this would've happened if you'd been fully on board. Your anal-retentive ass would've known how every penny was spent."

Damn straight. "I'm not sure where the money went, but I know one thing."

"You're going to do whatever it takes to find the bastards and hang them by the balls?"

Lanelle smiled at her friend's crassness. "What you said was better than I could've phrased it. I'm going to have to hold another fund-raiser. If I don't, the money comes from my pocket."

"You've already sunk how many millions into it?"

Lanelle had no issues with the money she'd invested to see the project completed. Technically, Eliana Lanelle Gill Astacio, the official name on her birth certificate, the only daughter and middle child of the Fortune 500 business tycoon who hailed from a lineage of Spanish royalty, had donated the money.

Having learned her older brother's experiences, Lanelle's parents had registered her in boarding school by her middle names. She'd become a Murphy when she got married and had kept the name when they divorced. Living a life outside the spotlight the Astacio name brought had suited her over the years.

When Lanelle had been asked to be on the board of the five-hundred-bed hospital two years ago, she'd noticed the NICU was inadequate. The tug on her heart to construct a larger, more modern unit pulled on her so hard she'd decided to spearhead the construction of one for the hospital.

The board had unanimously agreed to her proposal. After brainstorming, they'd designed a three-story structure. The top floor would consist of a hostel where parents could reside and still be near their babies.

The first floor would house the women who'd just delivered their premature or sick newborns. Lanelle had learned from experience that being on the same unit with happy mothers who got to take their adorable, gurgling children home with them in a couple of days added to mothers' depression when they couldn't do the same. Placing these women on their own floor while their child struggled to live would be a psychological boon. The second floor would consist of a state-of-the-art neonatal intensive care unit.

"Yeah. I'm sure Dad will shake his head in disappointment if I put in any more cash. And you know what Leonardo would say."

"He's an ass. Why does his opinion matter to you?"

"He's my older brother. He's gained a reputation as a cutthroat corporate lawyer, all without using my father's influence. I have to respect that."

"I'm not arguing with you about this again."

"He can be a pain sometimes."

Toshia arched an eyebrow. "Whenever I came to your house during school breaks, he'd torment me as much as he did you."

"He's misunderstood. I still say he's a good guy, on the rare occasion."

"How do you have the ability to see the good in everyone?" For once Toshia hadn't asked the question as if it was a curse.

Getting them back on course, Lanelle said, "I'm pretty sure the hospital won't infuse more money into the project, not when they've capped out what they'd anticipated giving. I haven't run it past the board yet, but I'm thinking of having one last fund-raiser. If we don't make enough, then I'll offset the costs." She upped the speed of the treadmill to help tame the distress storming through her. Over the past few years, it seemed like the universe had decided that, by any means necessary, she had to learn people couldn't be trusted. Letting her compassionate heart rule her life had led to some major disappointments. Without fail, she'd always decided to help rather than hide. If she could only maintain a more cynical frame of mind in which, like Toshia, she anticipated that people would screw her over.

The NICU had to get built, and she'd do anything to make it happen, even stomp down the people trying to get in the way.

"If you want, I'll donate my time to organize it."

Lanelle stopped short of jumping off the treadmill to hug her friend. "I couldn't thank you enough." Toshia was one of the most renowned party planners in the business. She'd organized all of the other successful fund-raisers they'd had for the hospital. For Toshia to offer her services for free went beyond the call of friendship.

"I can't let you be the only one doing your part to make the world a better place. When are you thinking of holding it?"

"In a month."

Toshia sucked air in through her teeth. "You're cutting it close."

"Yes, but I have the best event planner on board. Even if I gave you two days, you'd turn out a fabulous party."

"True." Toshia blew on her nails and rubbed them on her sopping-wet tank top with a smirk. "I am that good. When are you meeting with the board?"

"We're having an emergency meeting on Monday."

Toshia increased the pace on the StairMaster. "Be honest—what do you think is going on with the money?"

"I don't know. All of the paperwork looks good. And you know me."

"You can't think the worst about anybody until they show their true face." Toshia shook her head. "Not one of the traits I admire, by the way."

Lanelle grunted hard through her panting. She wouldn't get into it again about their personality differences, but if she were more untrusting she could circumvent some of the problems she'd had in her life before they even happened. But then she'd miss some of the good in people. "Maybe we just did some bad financial calculations."

"With you, Miss Graduated-with-Her-MBA-at-the-Top-of-Her-Class, as the head of the project, I doubt it. You're a natural-born philanthropist. When you aren't helping someone in need, you're computing to make sure your projects get the most out of what you have to offer."

"Other than setting the budget, the board doesn't deal with the money aspect. We only oversee that the decisions we've made are going in the right direction. If I'd been around, I would've kept a closer eye on things."

"Then you need to vet the hospital's accounting department. Brad's told me horror stories about what accountants have tried to do with his money." Toshia loved to talk about her husband even more than parties or clothes. "But because my baby is too smart to get taken, he circumvented their efforts. I'm sure the money is disappearing somewhere it's not supposed to."

The same suspicions had plagued Lanelle. "I've been there and found nothing. Wherever the funds went, they made a clean getaway." *For now.* No longer wanting to discuss her failure in keeping her project on course without a major glitch, Lanelle got lost in the music coming through her headphones.

Toshia knocked on the treadmill to capture Lanelle's attention. "You've gone to the previous fund-raisers alone. I *refuse* to let you do it again. Who are you taking as a date?" Toshia answered her own question. "How about Mr. Tall, Dark and Afro? I can't believe you fobbed him off."

The exact same thoughts had kept her tossing and turning the night away. Images of Dante had refused to leave as they morphed into fantasies about more than just their hands touching.

Lord knew she was long overdue for a good time.

"Why didn't you say yes to a date? The way you described him, he seems like a nice guy. You're the most instinctive person I know. Something told you to say yes, and yet you did the opposite. Inquiring Toshia wants to know why."

"You already do."

"Girl, you need to get over it. Your ex-husband was all kinds of a jerk for leaving you." She paused to catch her breath. "Not all men are the same. Conrad was a punk of distended proportions."

The loss of Lanelle's five-month-old baby as a stillbirth had devastated her. She'd survived the heartbreak and had gotten pregnant a year later, only to deliver premature twins and watch them die. She'd been distraught and beyond comfort. When she'd held their lifeless forms in her arms, she'd been told they'd suffered a severe case of anemia from her body attacking the babies' red blood cells.

Her B-negative blood lacked the rhesus, or Rh, factor; her first baby had inherited it from her ex-husband and tested positive for it after she'd miscarried. She'd been injected with the RhoGAM vaccine; if she didn't take the medication, her body would see the blood of the next Rh-positive child as a foreign body that had to be destroyed.

But the RhoGAM had failed, a rare occurrence that had stumped her obstetrician. The antibodies the vaccine was supposed to prevent her from developing had killed her twins.

Her ex-husband hadn't been able to handle the news that they'd most likely never have a child together, so he'd divorced her.

In less than two years, she'd had to suffer the tragic loss of her three children and had been left by a man who'd promised to stay with her through sickness and health. A childless marriage hadn't been part of the vows, so he'd taken off.

Lanelle would never be able to endure the agony of losing another child. Compounded with the fact that no matter how much a man claimed to love a woman, he couldn't be trusted to stay when he was needed. What was the point in having a relationship if he'd end up leaving?

Other than the occasional date forced on to her by her parents, her younger brother, Miguel, and Toshia, Lanelle hadn't had a long-term relationship since her ex-husband, Conrad, left her.

When she'd found out he and his new wife had delivered a healthy, full-term baby boy six months after they'd married, her heart had broken all over again. And her resolve to stay away from men had strengthened.

Lanelle had been pleased with her life choice to live like a nun. Until yesterday. Dante's knee-buckling smile started shattering walls she'd never intended to let crack.

"What's his name again?"

An image of his rich, dark skin came to mind. "Dante Sanderson."

Toshia pushed a button on the machine and stopped pumping her legs as it came to a stop. "Oh, my goodness, you like him."

"No, I don't."

"Alleluia, praise the Lord." Her friend raised both hands. "After all these years, she likes someone. Glory be. I know you like him," Toshia said. "It's the sappy smile that crept onto your face when you mentioned his name. And you said it all breathy."

"Couldn't be because I'm running on a treadmill at eight miles an hour."

"Go out with him."

Lanelle pressed the button to add an incline to her jog. "Even if I wanted to, which I don't, I couldn't."

Toshia crossed her arms over her full bosom. "Why the hell not?"

Lanelle pulled the first excuse that came to mind. "I don't have his number."

"Oh, please. It doesn't take the CIA to find someone. You have his first and last name. Look him up."

Tired of trying to justify her decision, Lanelle said, "If we meet again by chance, then I'll go out with him. If not, then it wasn't meant to be."

Toshia flattened her lips. "You don't believe in fate. Why would you bring it to the table with the first guy you've been attracted to in years?"

Because he scares me. "He seemed like too much of a smooth talker to trust."

"I can't believe you." Toshia glared at her. "That's not the reason, and you know it. It's been ages. When will you be ready to date again?"

Lanelle stopped the machine without going through a cooldown. "Time for weights."

"Fine, we'll talk about this later."

With Toshia's penchant for focusing on herself when prompted, Lanelle had no doubt they wouldn't speak about it for weeks to come. By then Dante Sanderson would no longer star in her fantasies.

Chapter 4

The most recent meeting Lanelle had with the hospital board dragged on for hours as they'd discussed the issue of funding for the NICU.

During the first half hour, tempers rose as some of the board members' anger about the lack of funds surfaced. Lanelle observed the discussion with a critical eye as she fumed. She couldn't believe there were some who seemed ambivalent to the miscalculations. And yet she didn't trust those being most vociferous in their outrage, either.

She ensured that her voice was calm when she said, "The best thing to do at this point is hire a forensic accountant to find out what happened to the money."

Rather than the commendation she expected for her idea, the room went silent. After a few seconds, one of the ones who hadn't seemed to care one way or the other said, "Forensic accountants are specialists who charge a lot of money for their work." She raised her eyebrow in a condescending way that made Lanelle's hand form a fist. "And who do you suppose should pay for it?"

Some of the others grumbled things Lanelle couldn't hear, which made her angrier because they seemed in support of the older woman. "If money has been stolen, they've done such a good job of it that it's probably not the first time. Wouldn't it be better to invest in finding out if funds are being stolen from the hospital?"

A couple people drank from the glasses that sat in front of them, increasing Lanelle's suspicions of some of their involvement.

"It's just conjecture that the money has been stolen. Any number of things could've happened to it," one of the others in the neutral camp said.

Incredulous, Lanelle calmed herself with a deep breath. "And that's why we need forensics to assess the situation. We need to know for sure what happened to the money."

The board's treasurer straightened his stack of papers. "You have an excellent point. But the question remains about funding the fees of the accountant." He paused as some of the members nodded. The smile, meant to charm her, didn't work. "Can I suggest another fund-raiser to off-set the remaining costs of this noble project you and your family have invested so generously toward?"

Lanelle's heart beat double time and she struggled to keep herself from shouting out her wrath. It would've hindered rather than helped. They already saw her as an eccentric rich woman from the powerful Astacio family, so they treated her very carefully. No need to add *crazy* to the list. "I hope we revisit the idea of hiring the forensic accountant." She settled her gaze on each of the board members as she vowed to discover the truth, even if she had to do it on her own. "My family would hate to think that their money has been allowed to be stolen due to…personal interests." Turning the tables in a flash, she smiled at the treasurer. "A fund-raiser would be a lovely idea."

Once the throat clearing, body shifting and water drinking settled down, they discussed the fund-raiser, which they all agreed Lanelle would chair and organize, as she'd expected. They'd hold the event in one month to try to keep on the building's work schedule while giving them time to plan.

Other than her suspicions of the involvement of some of the board members in stealing the project's money, the meeting went well once the tension dissipated. When it was adjourned, Lanelle had a clear plan in mind about both the fund-raiser and finding the money.

Grabbing her things, she left without making small talk with anyone and headed down to the hospital cafeteria for her favorite decadent treat. Her heart skipped a beat at the memory of meeting Dante the last time she'd gone there. She felt a niggling regret at not saying yes to his invitation. Recalling the children she'd always love but never hold and how she'd never put herself through that again, she knew saying no had been for the best.

Lanelle had been busy planning the fund-raiser with Toshia over the past couple weeks. Her friend had performed miracles to get the event organized.

At a meeting at Lanelle's house, they arranged a silent auction to help bring in more proceeds.

"We're ahead of schedule. Two more weeks and we can set this party off." Toshia leaned her elbows against Lanelle's desk. "So tell me what happened at the meeting with the forensic accountant."

"You will not believe how much money those people make." The quote had staggered her. "It will be worth it, though. I can't stand when people get away with doing the wrong thing."

"Not even your best friend." Toshia waggled her index finger. "You're not the one I'd ever call to help me bury a body. I'd end up in jail when you called the police."

Lanelle laughed. "Good thing I know you'd never kill anyone."

"If you say so." Toshia finished her drink and quirked

an eyebrow. "Did you set up a date with Mr. Afro for your fund-raiser?"

Something in Lanelle's belly fluttered at the mention of Dante. He'd been on her mind every day since they'd met. He epitomized the phrase "tall, dark and handsome" and she liked the confident manner and sense of humor he'd displayed during their much too short time together. How could she miss someone she'd known for less than fifteen minutes?

"I haven't seen or heard from him since the parking lot, so no." Although she'd seen a lot of him in her fantasies.

Toshia clucked her tongue. "You are one hard-headed woman. You know you liked him. Why don't you just get in contact with him? Brad thinks he's a good guy." Her face perked up. "I'll call him for you and set up a meeting." Her friend giggled. "It'll be destiny."

Lanelle gasped. She wasn't sure if she wanted Toshia to go through with her idea or not. Then the fear overtook her desire to get to know the first man she'd been attracted to in years. "Don't you dare, Toshia. Promise me that you won't."

Toshia pouted.

"Promise me."

"Fine," she said with more than a little petulance in her voice. "I've got to get going. I have a meeting across town in thirty minutes with a client. Get this—he wants to hold a five-story party with each floor having its own theme." Toshia glowed. "It's going to be my masterpiece."

Lanelle smiled at her friend's joy. "I'm happy for you." She walked Toshia to her car and hugged her goodbye. Just as Lanelle stepped into her house, her cell phone rang. At the name flashing on her phone, she smiled and answered. "Hello."

"Hi, Lanelle." Then a pause. "It's me, Vanessa."

They'd spoken almost every day since they'd met. She'd

even taken Vanessa out to dinner. Lanelle couldn't understand how they'd become fast friends in such a short time. The girl's intelligence, sense of humor and zest for life fascinated her, even though she found their connection disconcerting. The young lady had become the little sister she'd never known she'd wanted. "Why would you think I haven't saved your number? How'd class go this morning?"

"I think I'm going to change my major."

Having grown up with a business magnate for a father, one she'd emulated, Lanelle had known what she'd study long before she went to college. She'd never wavered in her decision and couldn't understand how Vanessa had changed majors three times. "Again?"

"I'm having a hard time making up my mind."

Lanelle had nothing scheduled for the day except her weekly video chat to keep in touch with her parents when they traveled. She could postpone it to the evening. For once they'd taken a trip to Jamaica to unwind, rather than for business.

She made a quick decision. Hanging out with Vanessa was like blowing bubbles: fun, light and easy. The young woman posed no threat. Her uncle, on the other hand…

"How about I pick you up for lunch and we'll talk about it?"

"Sounds good. I'll be waiting in front of the building with the golden dome like last time. Are you taking me to Azure again? Wait. How about I take you to lunch this time?"

"You're a student. I'm not in the mood for Burger King."

The harrumph of annoyance would've been more believable if not followed by a chuckle. "Goes to show what you know. I would've taken you to Wendy's. Their value meals are better."

"Since I invited you, I'll choose the place."

"I don't care where we go—food is food."

Said like a true college student. "I'll be there in thirty. Bye."

Every time she agreed to meet Vanessa, Lanelle wondered if Dante would show up. It unnerved her that she wanted to see him again. After two weeks, she hadn't been able to get him off her mind. A man Vanessa adored couldn't be a bad guy.

The thrill of awareness she'd felt when he'd touched her had been unparalleled. She sighed. Maybe if she'd met Dante before her life had gone to hell, something good could've come from getting to know him. At this point, she could let no man in, not even a handsome, muscular, charming one who'd stolen her breath and ingrained himself into her daily thoughts.

In the middle of picking out his tuxedo for a fundraising event two weeks from Saturday, Dante's phone rang. He excused himself from the tailor after looking at the screen.

He'd barely gotten out his hello when his niece shouted, "Get to campus right now. Lanelle's picking me up in twenty-eight minutes."

"What happened to not telling me where she'd be?"

"That was before I realized you'd be perfect for each other."

Besides their initial two chance meetings, Dante hadn't run into Lanelle again. He knew nothing about her other than that she possessed the wit and intelligence he'd observed during those brief encounters. Over the past couple of weeks, an image of her beautiful face would pop into his mind at random. When he remembered the spark in her eyes when they'd touched, his skin would get flushed. Not a day went by when he didn't regret not pushing her for a date, but she seemed as stubborn as he tended to be tenacious, so he'd played the game by her rules. "What makes you think so?"

"I'm not going to say. I just know. Are you coming down?"

And have her call me a cheater and renege on the offer of a date? No. "I'm in the middle of a tuxedo fitting."

"Can't you do it later?"

The salesman tapped his foot as he leaned against the counter. "I'll be out of town for a couple of weeks. I'll be back just in time to attend a formal fund-raising dinner I've been invited to. If I don't get fitted now, then I'll be wearing a suit to the dinner."

"Where are you off to now? I thought you gave most of your travel assignments to one of your executives."

His niece had a knack for remembering things he'd never expect her to, especially when it came to his work.

"Is it Italy?" She sounded so excited Dante chuckled. "Can I go with you?"

Vanessa had been hounding him for a trip ever since she'd been a little girl. Maybe he'd have to make her dream come to fruition. After the cancer scare, he knew life, no matter the person's age, could be gone in a moment. "Listen, I've got to go. Have a good time with Lanelle. As she said, if it's meant to be, it will be."

Vanessa sucked her teeth. "That philosophy is bogus. I like it better when you say that if you want something, go out and get it. What changed your mind?"

I don't want to piss her off and mess up a chance to get to know her. "I'll talk to you later."

"Bye."

Dante turned to the salesman. "I'm ready."

Lanelle had starred in all of his fantasies since meeting her. It wouldn't mean as much if they'd all been sexual. When he'd imagined them having a conversation over dinner, he knew she'd affected him more than a woman he'd just met should've. And yet he hadn't made a move toward finding her. He'd give it more time. Maybe a month. If they didn't meet by then, he'd do what was more in line with his nature and make it happen.

In the meantime, he'd focus on his business. The hospital project had fallen into his lap, the perfect way to try his hand at a new type of flooring. This contract marked the beginning of a new era in his company. Once they completed the job to perfection, the referrals would flood in. Then he'd be able to get the wicked and greedy Calvano clan off his back.

He ground his teeth at the thought of losing part of his business to them. A deep breath helped to clear the anger. With this hospital bid in his pocket, he no longer had to worry. He'd beat the deadline and maintain complete control of his company.

Perhaps the only thing that would rank with beating the Calvanos would be dating Lanelle.

Chapter 5

Everything at the fund-raiser was perfect, from the food to the elegantly dressed patrons who'd donated generously to be part of the event. Of course it had helped that she'd let it leak that her paparazzi-beloved brother, Miguel, would attend. He loved the limelight more than Lanelle did her privacy. She watched her brother schmooze his way through the guests, encouraging them to further support the NICU by bidding in the silent auction they'd planned.

"I wish Mom and Dad could be here to see what a wonderful job you've done," Lanelle gushed as she took in the splendor of the ballroom. "Toshia, you've outdone yourself."

"Thanks. I tried to create a glamorous space without going crazy with the budget. Where are your parents now?"

"You know them. They said they went to Jamaica to relax, but after a week they took off to the Dominican Republic for a tour of their sugarcane plantations and manufacturing company. Then they're going to Columbia to check on their coffee investment."

Toshia shook her head. "What aren't your parents into?"

Lanelle rolled her eyes up and to the right, pretending

to think. "Staying in one place for too long, and drugs. Wait, let me clarify. Illegal drugs. They do own a pharmaceutical company."

Her friend dropped a piece of fresh cantaloupe wrapped in prosciutto onto her plate. "Good job getting Miguel to come."

She smiled as she found her younger brother laughing with a politically prominent man. Miguel was the antithesis of their oldest sibling, always seeking fun, while Leonardo took life much too seriously "I didn't even bother to invite Leonardo. He would've claimed to be busy with work, and I wasn't up for the rejection."

Toshia didn't hide her frown at Lanelle's antisocial brother's behavior. "How far has the forensic accountant come with the investigation?"

Lanelle shook her head. "Nothing yet. He's thorough, too. He's inquired into the contractors we used, but he hasn't found anything out of the normal. It's not as if anyone is going to confess to stealing the money, so it might take some deep digging to find out what we need. I still find it impossible to believe someone would embezzle from a hospital. Or at all, for that matter."

Toshia sucked her teeth. "First of all, you are such a sucker. You believe everyone is inherently good and all that crap."

"Toshia!"

She ignored the outburst. "Secondly, we've always had money, so we never had to worry. You'd be surprised at what people will do to obtain it." Toshia took a delicate bite of the meat-and-fruit combination. "Why don't you ask your parents, or even Leonardo, for help?"

Lanelle picked up a glass of champagne from a passing waiter and took a sip before placing it on the table. Her churning stomach hadn't allowed her to eat much at dinner, so she needed to take it easy on the alcohol. "I can handle it."

"If you say so." Toshia blew a kiss to someone across the room.

Lanelle turned to see a tall, broad-shouldered man headed their way.

"Brad and I are going to leave soon. Since the party's winding down, there's no need for me to stay. The caterers have their instructions."

Toshia's husband slipped an arm around her waist, bent down and whispered something in her ear, eliciting a girlish giggle.

The tiniest stab of jealousy made Lanelle avert her gaze from the happy couple. Five years of marriage and they still got so wrapped up in each other that no one else in the room existed.

Through the good and the bad, Brad had stuck by Toshia's side. Lanelle considered him to be a different breed of man from the rest. *How can you classify all men as the same when you don't get to know any of them? Just like Brad, not all of them are weak. Great. Now my subconscious sounds just like Toshia's blabbing.*

Lanelle's sharp inhale drew the lovebirds' attention as her gaze settled on the one person she'd never expected to see again. Too late to turn and hide behind Brad. True to her obstinate nature, she hadn't come with a date, so she had no one to use as an excuse.

The slow saunter of slim hips, emphasized by powerful, tuxedo-clad shoulders, captivated Lanelle. She raked her gaze from his shiny black shoes up to his magnificent body to meet his eyes. With a single look, the man held her frozen, stopping her from running for her life.

Lanelle resisted the urge to look down at her gold taffeta dress to make sure her hardened nipples weren't poking through. Just in case, she crossed her arms over her breasts. With an ease that told of his utmost confidence, Dante reached for one of her hands and placed a kiss on her knuckles.

"What a *coincidence* to see you again, Lanelle." He tucked her hand into the crook of his left arm. She made a pathetic attempt to extract it, but the little tug ended up being useless.

"Won't you introduce us to your friend?" Toshia's voice had risen a pitch.

Shifting her gaze from Dante's glittering light brown eyes, Lanelle felt the party filter back into her consciousness.

Clearing her throat in an attempt to gain a few seconds to compose herself, Lanelle plastered on a smile before making the introductions. "This is my best friend, Toshia, and her husband, Bradley Covington. This is—"

"Dante Sanderson." Brad held out his hand.

"Good to see you again."

Toshia's mouth dropped open. "How do you two know each other?" Toshia asked.

Brad encircled his wife's waist. "We've worked together on a few projects. He's excellent when it comes to supplying and installing top-quality marble and granite."

"I've branched into PVC floor installation."

"PVC?" Toshia asked.

"It stands for polyvinyl chloride," Lanelle answered. "They use it for plastic pipes and flooring. It can be created to look like wood, linoleum or anything in between. Depending on the look you want. You know the flooring they use in the gym? That's PVC. It's a rather versatile material."

Dante turned to her with his eyebrows raised.

"What?" No need to tell him she'd come about the information while doing research on what type of flooring would be best for a hospital. "I can't know things?"

Dante flexed his biceps in response. "I'm pretty sure you know a whole lot."

Lanelle's intake of breath didn't go unnoticed by her friend as Toshia smirked.

"Brad, if you have a project that needs vinyl, give me a call. And you know I'm always available for marble and granite."

"I'll be sure to do that."

Lanelle found it impossible to calm her racing heart.

"Isn't the world just too small, Lanelle?" Toshia asked.

"As a Ping-Pong ball," Lanelle creaked out, placing a hand to her throat as she struggled to swallow. Where was a wandering champagne waiter when she needed one? Darn their competence at picking up her first glass. "I need a drink."

Lanelle released her arm from Dante's prison and pivoted toward the bar.

"I'll join you. We'll catch up later during the evening, Brad."

"Toshia and I are leaving, but I'll give you a call."

Lanelle reached one of the strategically located bars within seconds. She forced a smile at the bartender. "Gin and tonic. Not too much ice, please." She didn't hear what Dante ordered and didn't care. When the cold drink hit her hand, she downed half of it in gulps.

She glared at Dante. "What are you doing here?"

"I hope someone's told you how stunning you look tonight."

Taking a step back from his magnetism didn't help. "Flattering me isn't an answer to the question. Did Vanessa tell you I'd be here?" Too late, she recalled she hadn't told Vanessa anything about tonight.

"It's good to know you're a little paranoid before we go out on our date." A slow, sexy grin made an unwarranted appearance, weakening her knees. "I thought I'd imagined your graceful beauty, but my memory didn't do you justice."

Lanelle lifted her straight shoulder-length hair off her neck, wishing she'd worn it in an updo so she wouldn't feel so overheated. "Still not an answer."

He took a sip of the dark drink he'd ordered, placed it on the counter and then took her glass.

"Hey, I was drinking that."

"For the record, I had no idea you'd be here, so you can calm down. If you dance with me, I'll explain my presence at this," he lowered his voice, "rather boring party."

She wouldn't be able to withstand being so close to him. Even now his scent enticed her, drawing her closer. "Or…" She poked him in his chest, only to wince at the pain she'd caused herself. "You could save us the trouble of going to the dance floor and explain it here and now while I finish my drink."

Dante held out his arm. The man was an enigma. Showing up at a last-minute fund-raiser gala. Late, too, because she was pretty sure she would've noticed him earlier. Plus, he knew Brad.

The fact that he caused her body to react in incredible ways she could never recall happening before was beside the point. She had information to ascertain, and she would. Placing her hand in the crook of his arm, she went with him to the dance floor.

The space he maintained between them as they danced to a smooth jazz song should've helped her to relax. Her gaze roamed the still-crowded ballroom. With the help of a few friends, she'd organized a silent auction. From the bids she'd seen earlier in the night, the guests had been generous.

Her brother came into sight. She wasn't happy about the wink he sent her. Miguel could see romance in anything. Sometimes a dance with a man who set her insides on fire with his touch was just a dance.

Without warning, Dante invaded her space and tilted her into a dip. Gripping the shoulder of his tuxedo, she scowled into his smiling face as the blood rushed to her head. Before she could chastise him, he brought her upright.

She hated surprises. Being out of control ranked number one on her never-to-do list. Dante threatened all of that. From the few stories Vanessa had told about him, they were as different as a waltz and a tango. "Talk."

Should she be feeling the deep rumble of his laughter against her chest? When had he pulled her so close? She tried to re-create space between them. His hand splayed against her back made it impossible.

"Do you ever loosen up?"

She snapped her head up. Even though she was wearing stilettoes, he loomed over her. "You've met me what, all of twice? You have no idea who I am."

He leaned in, his breath tickling her ear as he whispered, "But I'd like to."

All thoughts of why she'd come on the dance floor escaped as he pressed his cheek against hers. For once in her life, Lanelle lost herself in the gentle sway of a man's embrace.

Chapter 6

Dante willed the music to play forever. Once Lanelle let go of her stiff and demanding demeanor and melted into him, everything changed.

Her tall, lithe frame fit well into his. For those precious moments they formed a fluid connection. When the song ended, they continued with the same languorous movements, which could barely be interpreted as dancing.

An up-tempo beat blared through the system. Hesitant to distance himself from Lanelle's sweet rose scent and perfect body, he summoned his strength and took a step back. Pleased it took her a few seconds to lift her eyelids, he angled himself farther back, though that didn't dim the need to kiss her. But at least it made her less accessible.

"Unless we want to swing dance, we should get off the floor."

She broke eye contact first. For a moment he thought she'd break out into dance when she tapped her foot to the tune before walking away.

Caught up in her essence, he had no choice but to follow.

This time at the bar she ordered sparkling water as she slipped onto the stool. After her first sip, she raised an eyebrow. Needing no further prompting, Dante said, "I'm doing work for the hospital. When they sent me the invitation, I thought it would be a good way to network."

"At a thousand dollars a plate?"

He hoped the lift of his shoulder exhibited the nonchalance he attempted to portray. Lanelle had his insides tied in knots. *What is it about her?* "I figure it's for a good cause. Besides, I'm doing the flooring on the hospital wing they threw this fund-raiser for."

Lanelle's hand fluttered to her throat, and a soft "oh" came out.

Dante expected her to say more after such a strange reaction. "And what brings you here?" he asked when she remained quiet.

Her eyes widened the slightest bit before she stated, "Toshia planned this event, and I wanted to support her. Didn't she do a brilliant job?" Lanelle held up a hand to the side of her mouth and stage-whispered, "I happen to know she did it under budget. So if you're looking for an event planner, you might want to give Toshia a try."

Those words had to be the most she'd said to him at one time. The woman was too couth to babble. And yet she had. Maybe he'd misjudged her. *Or she's hiding something.*

The drink in Lanelle's hand disappeared as she drained it. When ice cubes remained, she sucked one in and chewed.

He clenched his teeth together as the sound grated in his ears. He must've winced because she stopped and covered her mouth. "I'm sorry. I didn't mean to annoy you."

"How could you have known listening to someone chew ice is worse than nails on a chalkboard for me?"

"Do they make those anymore?"

"I'm not sure. All I remember is my classmates using it as a form of torture when they went to the board."

"Did you ever have to clap the erasers?"

He chuckled at the memories that dredged up. "It was my favorite job. I loved creating a cloud of chalk dust. Plus, it got me out of the classroom."

She scrunched her nose. "I hated it. The teacher would make me do it as a punishment."

"For what? You don't seem like the kind of person who'd get into any sort of trouble."

"You'd be surprised."

Their gazes held. *I'm sure I would be.* He couldn't let her slip away again. Vanessa wouldn't be the only one who got the chance to enjoy her company. "About our date. Are you free tomorrow?"

A flicker of her eyes to the right and upward told him she was about to lie. He hated liars. Before she could speak, he reminded her, "Destiny has brought us together. You owe me a date. You said it yourself in the parking lot."

"Tomorrow is Sunday."

"And? We could do something fun."

Lanelle lifted her glass, and just as she opened her mouth to take a piece of ice, she stopped and placed it on the bar, pushing it away. With less enthusiasm than he would've liked, she asked, "What time?"

"Will you be going to church tomorrow?"

"Yes."

"What time does the service end?"

"Ten."

Dante chuckled. "No all-day worship for you?"

Lanelle smiled. "I'm good with a couple of hours."

"Me, too. How about if I pick you up at eleven? We could go to brunch."

Her dramatic sigh made him think she'd rather dip her toe in a pond filled with crocodiles than go out with him. "How about we meet somewhere? At the restaurant would be good."

"Ever been to Peaches 'n' Cream?"

"Yes." She hopped off the bar stool. "See you there tomorrow at eleven." Backing up a step, she hitched a thumb over her shoulder. "I promised I'd take care of some things for Toshia so she could leave early with her husband."

"Are you an event planner, too?"

"With my anal-retentive organizational skills, I could be, but no."

"What do you do?"

The step she was about to take faltered, and Dante reached out to steady her. He couldn't help himself from bending his head toward her when her gaze dropped to his lips. Enticed by the heat from her silky skin, he caressed her arm. Clasping a hand at the back of her neck, he went for what he'd been dreaming about since he'd first met her.

Before he could reach his goal, he yelped in pain. Without drawing attention to them, Lanelle held his pinkie in some kind of death grip.

He hissed in a breath when she made the tiniest move to the left. "That hurts."

Her lips curled up in a vicious smile. "I know. Do you remember what I told you when we first met?"

No thought other than getting his finger out of her mean grip came to mind. "Refresh my memory," he gritted out. To the crowd, they must have looked like a normal couple, touching in an almost intimate way. The control she had over him with just his pinkie in her possession humbled more than embarrassed him. "Can you please let go, first?"

She did as he asked. He massaged his poor finger behind his back. As the pain diminished, the memory surfaced. "You said you could take me down."

"Yes. And you didn't believe it. I'd appreciate if you didn't touch me again." She angled her head in a silent warning.

Her reaction had been extreme. She could've told him

no and he would've backed off. What had happened in her life to make her use violence as a first resort? Or was she one of those women who'd rather fight than communicate?

He could explain he'd touched her only to ensure her safety. But it would be a lie. It may have started that way, but it had transitioned into more. He'd been about to kiss her.

Even now, knowing she could land him on the floor without breaking a sweat, he wanted to swipe a lock of hair off her forehead, and her lips still beckoned. Would they be as soft as her cheek had been against his while they'd danced? *Softer,* his brain teased.

How could he keep the promise he was about to make? "As you wish."

A curt nod and she left. If only she'd take the throbbing in his pinkie and the need to hold her again with her.

Would her legs support her? Still shaken from the encounter with the sexiest man on the planet, Lanelle barely made it to the auction table. She placed her hands against it to help support her weight. Her knees seemed to have changed consistency.

What got into me? She shook her head, attempting to figure out if she was more upset about almost kissing Dante or preventing it from happening. Causing him pain had been her instinctive reaction to stop her from making a colossal mistake. She didn't need a man. Especially one who seemed to move through life on so much testosterone it formed a cloud around him.

She had no excuse for attacking him, other than pure terror at wanting his kiss so much. She'd panicked and she hated that she'd been driven to it.

Her little self-defense move should've made him cancel their date. Who wanted to go out with an unpredictable woman who spouted off about destiny? Obviously Dante did. Maybe she should reassess him.

If she were to date again, it would be with someone predictable. Someone she could depend on to support her, even when life became so demanding they'd wonder if they'd make it through. Yet they'd buoy each other, knowing they'd survive any problem attempting to plow them over.

No such man existed. She preferred the thought of being alone for the rest of her life over getting her heart broken again. Especially when she wouldn't give him children.

A hand at the small of her back preceded a deep voice asking, "Are you okay?"

She jumped and turned with her arms in a defensive position. She relaxed when Miguel came into view. She had to calm down; otherwise, she'd put someone in the hospital.

Miguel held both hands up. "Sorry. I didn't mean to scare you."

Lanelle admired her brother's handsome face. She could see why the cameras and women loved him. She used to love braiding his soft, curly hair when they were younger. Now the ringlets falling over his forehead brought out the onyx color of his eyes. "You know how I am with surprises."

Miguel's smile displayed a double onslaught of dimples. "You detest them. Who was the guy you were dancing with? You two looked cozy."

"Just a guy I met a month ago at the hospital." Simple and to the point.

Miguel stroked his goatee. "Hmm. Then why'd you have him in one of your infamous pinkie grips when he got a little close?"

Mortified, Lanelle covered her face with both hands

and groaned. She could've ruined the whole party with her impetuous maneuver. Miguel pulled her hands down. "You used that move on me so many times I can recognize it anywhere. No one else even noticed." He tipped her chin upward so she had to look him in the eyes. "Not that it wasn't funny as hell to see it happening to someone else for once, but what ticked you off that much?"

"Nothing," she said. Other than Dante's attempt to give her the kiss she'd desired, up until the point when their lips had almost touched.

"Are you sure? He may look tough, but I think I could take him."

Lanelle laughed. "Thanks for the offer, but I'm good." To keep from telling him that she and Dante would be going on a date tomorrow, she said, "And thank you so much for being here tonight. Your presence made a huge impact."

Miguel blew on his nails and wiped them on his tuxedo jacket to polish them. "It's because I'm the man."

"More like the party boy of the tabloids."

He shrugged. "That, too."

She hugged Miguel with gratitude and love. When she pulled away, an uncomfortable chill shimmied down her spine. Lanelle looked toward the bar and found Dante watching her, his face expressionless. But even from this distance she could feel the coldness of his eyes. He had no right to be upset; they weren't dating. Then why did she feel like explaining that Miguel was her brother when she rarely told people she was an Astacio?

The man had her reacting in the strangest ways, and she couldn't have it. She was known as the levelheaded one in the family.

She sucked in a deep breath as she looked away from Dante's penetrating gaze. On their date tomorrow, she'd focus their conversations on his work at the hospital.

Maybe she'd gain some insight into the missing money. After that, they'd never see each other again.

She scoffed at the thought. The way things were going, they'd probably end up meeting each other on a daily basis until he wore her down. She had no doubt his overwhelming charm eventually would if they stayed in contact.

With him working on the NICU's floors, it might be difficult to avoid him when they did inspections. Maybe she'd get lucky and he wouldn't be around. Or would she be even luckier if he was?

Chapter 7

If Lanelle wanted space, then he'd create a chasm so wide it would take a jet to cross until she loosened up and wanted to close the distance. Why didn't he just cancel the date? Granted, he had no right to touch her last night without obtaining her permission, but there had been something powerful drawing them together. He thought she'd felt it, too. *Obviously not.*

Watching her the night before with Miguel Astacio didn't help.

Dante shook off the self-doubt. He hadn't imagined the attraction, yet he somehow knew she didn't want to like him.

This was why he never let women get under his skin anymore. They held all the power. It didn't take much for them to make a man crazy. Short-term relationships with little emotional attachments worked best for him. Anything else morphed into a disaster.

He refused to dwell on the relationship he'd had with his ex-fiancée in college, who'd claimed to love him but had only been using him while on campus. He'd learned way too late that when she went home, she hooked up with her rich boyfriend. He'd been wary of dating anyone for years after that.

Once he'd started earning some good money, women approached him. It had taken getting hurt a couple of times to realize that keeping things light was the best way to handle those encounters.

At five minutes to eleven, Dante stepped into the restaurant.

The hostess greeted him with a bright smile. "Hi, how many, please?"

"Table for two, please. My companion will be joining me shortly." Dante liked the sound of the sentence.

"Please follow me."

She led him to a table on the terrace, where they could enjoy the bright, sunny day. "The waiter will be with you in a moment."

Distracted as he'd been by Lanelle's heady perfume last night and the memory of the feel of her flush against him, phone numbers had been the last thing on his mind. So he'd neglected to get her number. By the time he'd thought about it, he'd stormed out of the ballroom, unable to stand watching her with another man.

Within moments, he looked up and saw the star of his fantasies scanning the room. Dante wiped his damp hands on his black trousers before standing to wave at her. Unlike with other women he'd met and dated, he had no idea how to behave around Lanelle. One wrong move could get him sent to the hospital. It would be worth it.

Be yourself, but don't touch her. Tempt her enough so she can't refuse another date with you. No problem.

His friends didn't call him a ladies' man for nothing. And then she stepped onto the terrace. His mouth dried at the sight of her within touching distance in a yellow-and-white polka-dot dress. He could barely remember his middle name, much less his manners, as she strode to the table. He just hoped he didn't embarrass himself.

No woman will ever get the best of you. Be cool and get what you want.

Lanelle didn't hear a single murmur of conversation in the restaurant as she approached the table. She wished Dante would stop whatever he was doing to make her heart speed up. How would she get through this brunch?

She found it impossible to tear her gaze away. God should seriously think about banning the combination of sharp features, light eyes, smooth, dark skin and a slow, sensual grin. A flash of what she'd missed last night as his full lips had come within inches of touching hers rent a moan of regret from her throat.

Maintaining a neutral expression in an attempt to avoid revealing her excitement at being near him, she nodded as he stood and pulled out her chair. "Good morning."

Dante held out his hand to Lanelle. She hesitated before reaching out. She braced herself for the anticipated electric shock that would follow his touch and wasn't disappointed when it happened. The warmth of their contact spread through her, and she had no desire to let go.

When he released her hand, she dropped it into her lap.

Before things could get too awkward between them, the waiter came and they ordered their drinks. As a unit, they went to the buffet line to get their food. Lanelle chose to have a specialty omelet of mushrooms, green peppers, onions and cheese made. While she waited for her food, she watched Dante load his plates. "You know you can come back for more, don't you?"

He chuckled. "You'd better believe I will, too."

He waited until her eggs had been cooked and then led her to their table.

As they ate, she racked her brain. She'd always prided

herself on her conversational skills. But today all thoughts other than the thrill of being near Dante again had vanished. The standard opener had to do. "It's a beautiful day."

He seemed to contemplate her as he finished chewing. "I can't argue. It's just that…"

"What?"

"Being with you outshines the day."

She swallowed hard. *Crap.*

Judging from how quiet Lanelle became during the meal after his compliment, Dante realized he may have laid it on a little too thick. "Listen. I know I may not have another opportunity to get to know you, so I wanted to dive into it." He let a slick grin slip onto his face. "If I don't like what you reveal, then I'll have no regrets if you never want to see me again."

"And if you like what I have to say?"

"Well, then, I'll have to make sure we go out again, won't I?"

She indicated toward his empty plates. "Are you going for more?"

Realizing how quickly their time together had flown, Dante rubbed his stomach. "I have just enough space for a slice of the crumb cake I noticed on the dessert table and a cup of coffee." He stood and offered his hand. "Interested in joining me?"

Lanelle stared at his hand for an interminable amount of time before pushing her chair back and grabbing it. Once she'd stood, she didn't let go, and neither did he. Tempted to walk out of the restaurant with the heat of her fingers wrapped around his rather than go to the dessert table, he enjoyed those precious moments as he took them to their destination.

He missed her touch when she let go and picked up a plate.

She perused the dessert table. "Since it's Sunday and the calories of all foods are half off, I'll go with a waffle slathered with chocolate ice cream and caramel syrup."

He laughed as he moved to the opposite end of the table, appreciating her sense of humor. "Would you like a cup of coffee with it?"

"No, thanks."

They assembled their goodies and went back to the table. Dante added sugar and milk to the coffee. "We're going to skip over all the general getting-to-know-you stuff and hit the good points. Since I want to impress you, I'll start. I can speak two languages fluently."

She looked up to see him holding up his middle and index finger. "Oh, really? I presume one is English."

"Yes. And the other is Italian."

She arched a brow.

"Are you impressed?"

She slathered a piece of waffle with ice cream and placed it in her mouth. "Am I supposed to be?"

"Um…yes."

"I would be if I didn't speak six languages."

"Fluently?"

She tucked a piece of her hair back behind her ear as if she hadn't meant to make the revelation. "I'd only speak them better if I were born in the country."

"If you don't speak Italian, then none of them count."

"Is that so?"

He slid the side of his fork into his cake and took a bite, enjoying its moist texture. "Since that conversation may lead to an argument, I'll provide you with another fun fact about me. I'm a fabulous lover."

The water she'd been drinking came spewing out of her mouth. Good thing she'd turned to the side before doing so; otherwise, he would've gotten another shower for the day.

Dante couldn't hold back his laughter. "It's true. If you want, I can demonstrate."

"I'll take your word for it." Wiping her mouth one last time, she said, "I've been bungee jumping."

Clever way to change the subject and pique his interest. "Was it on a dare?"

"I was the one who dared my friend to do it. She chickened out at the last moment."

"Interesting to know you were a risk taker in your younger years."

An unexpected grunt came from her. "Only if you consider last year the days of my youth."

Getting to know her would be fun. "I'm sure my whitewater rafting adventures in a level-five rapid would impress you."

"I am." She lay down her fork and rested her elbows on the table. "But how about jumping into the water from a moving helicopter?"

"Good one, but it can't top the most exhausting adventure I've ever had in my whole life."

Her adorable brows creased together. "And what was that?"

"Taking a trip to Disney World with *all* my nieces and nephews. You haven't experienced anything until you've run around The Greatest Place on Earth after jacking them up with sugar you had no idea you weren't supposed to give them. No experience could be crazier."

Lanelle's laughter pleased him. "I concede. You win."

And from that moment onward the conversation flowed, each trying to outdo the other with their experiences. Dante had never had such a fabulous first date, and he didn't want it to end.

Chapter 8

This had to be the best date Lanelle had ever been on. Dante cracked her up throughout their dessert with his willingness to share embarrassing stories about himself and his family.

There were some points when his eyes became intense, as if attempting to convey his desire to be alone with her. To finish the kiss she'd refused to share.

Stop projecting. Admit you want him to hold you against his hard body and kiss you. Be bold enough to go for what you want. It doesn't mean you'll marry him. You don't even have to fall in love—just enjoy what he has to offer.

More food and drink didn't appeal to her, but extending their time did. "I'm going for some tea. Would you like anything?"

A flash of mischief in his eyes told her his answer would be one of the shocking variety, but when he requested a second cup of coffee, she was disappointed he'd held back. She needed something to dislike about him so she could stop enjoying his company.

The heat of his eyes on her retreating back, most likely even lower, changed her gait. No one would consider her walk sexy, but she added a bit of swing to her hips as an enticement. Then she mentally slapped herself. Did she want to drive him away or keep him?

He met her halfway on her return trip to the table and took the saucers.

Not for the first time, Lanelle admired his gallant behavior. "Vanessa tells me you're taking her, the family and one of her friends on a trip to Italy for her twenty-first birthday."

A smile appeared at the mention of his niece. "She's been bugging me to go for years, and I tend to spoil my nieces and nephews."

She opened a packet of sugar and poured it in, along with a dash of milk. "I figured. I just hope no one vomits on this trip."

"With her seven-year-old brother, Ryan, joining us, there are no guarantees."

She took a tentative sip of the hot beverage before asking, "What made you choose Italy?"

"The choice was hers. She could've had anything she wanted. Within reason, of course."

"I can see why you added the stipulation."

He tapped his temple. "My parents didn't raise no fool."

Lanelle considered asking how successful he was at his job to be able to afford such an extravagant trip for six people. "She whined about only being able to invite a female friend because you barred any males from going. You know her best friend is a guy, right?"

A gleam entered his eyes. "Have you ever been to Italy?"

His clean-cut good looks were overwhelming. Lanelle picked up her cup at the sudden dryness of her throat. Afraid of what her voice would sound like, she shook her head.

"If she took a guy she even remotely likes as a guest, I promise they'll be head over heels in love midtrip."

Lanelle rested her chin on her hands. "Really? How do you know?"

"It's the most romantic country in the world," Dante answered as if it were the only possible response.

Unable to believe what the man had spouted, Lanelle shifted a little closer to see if he was serious. "I've traveled to countries with male friends while I was in college and nothing happened except enjoying the sights. France, Britain, Greece, Austria, Peru."

A muscle twitched in his jaw. "If you had gone to Italy, we wouldn't be having this discussion because you would've experienced it for yourself."

Her gut clenched. "Have you ever fallen in love with someone you've taken to Italy?"

Dante's dark eyes locked with hers for the longest moment. "I only go there for business. I've never taken anyone other than my executive staff with me before. And they were males."

"Oh." Lanelle let out a breath, slumping into the chair as if all the stress in the world had left her body. Why had his answer mattered so much?

The atmosphere shifted toward uncomfortable, and Lanelle took a huge sip of her tea. Time to end whatever they'd started. Gathering the strength to conclude the date, she halted her words when Dante spoke. "When was the last time you went to a fair?"

Lanelle blinked in rapid succession. "It's been at least twenty years."

He raised his hand to signal for their check. "Good. Then you should enjoy our little adventure this afternoon. Today is their last day. I was going to take Ryan and Vanessa, but my sister did yesterday. Ryan is still resting from all the fun and food he ate." He rubbed his hands together and grinned. "So are you up for the most excitement you'll have all day?"

Telling him how much interest she'd made on one of her financial portfolios this morning wouldn't endear her to him on the fun meter, so she countered with, "What if I have plans?"

"You can break them."

Cocky man. "What makes you think that's possible?"

He cocked his head. "You don't seem like you have a lot of fun on a daily basis. I'd like to balance that out a little." Then he winked. "And because you get to stay with me for a little longer. The way you've been wiping away your tears of mirth, I think I'm good for you to hang around." She admired his straightforwardness. No need to wonder where she stood with him, and she liked it. Too much. But she didn't want their time together to end so she said, "Let's go to the fair."

Burning rubber on a two-wheeled U-turn in his Suburban sounded better to Dante than taking Lanelle back to her car after the great time they'd had at the fair. To the best of his knowledge, kidnapping, even it if was merely to spend more time with her, was illegal in Ohio. And, oh, yes, the world.

His restraint when it came to touching her had been phenomenal, but he'd been no saint. With every incidental opening she'd given him, he dived in. On the Ferris wheel, he'd opened his legs wide so their knees touched. Things had gotten a little cheesy when he'd stood with his arms wrapped around her to help her aim at the water-pistol game. He'd sat in the perfect spot of all the spinning rides so she'd be glued to his side. They'd gone on each of those twice.

I need to see her again.

Lanelle's perpetual smile on the way back to the restaurant made him even happier he'd pushed to stay with her. "You mentioned flooring and doing work at the hospital," she said. "Who do you work for?"

Puffing out his chest, he would've strutted if they'd been outside. "Myself. I own the company." Why not boast a little? "The project my company will be working on is huge. A brand-new three-story neonatal wing. It's a big deal because it's different from anything I've worked on before."

She turned to him with her mouth agape. "What's the name of your business?"

"Calvano Flooring."

Dante spared her a glance when she responded with a gasp as her hand slapped her chest. She opened her mouth several times before she stuttered, "Cal… Cal… Calvano?"

"Yes. I maintained the name when the man I took over the business from died. Is something wrong, Lanelle? You don't seem to be breathing."

Never in a million years would she have suspected Dante's involvement with her passion project. *The name of his company is Italian, for goodness' sake.*

The procurement committee that had acquired the bids included three board members and four hospital staff. Ever since she'd found out money had been siphoned from the project, she regretted having had to decline being on the committee because she'd been too busy helping her father. Lanelle found out who won the bids only after the fact and had been shocked when Toshia's husband's company hadn't been chosen to do the construction. His work had the reputation of being top quality, efficient and moderate with the pricing.

Marble. Italian marble. Dante and Brad had discussed it at the fund-raiser. Even her father had mentioned doing business with Calvano Flooring when he'd built a hotel in Boston. Her dad had gone on about how he admired the perfection of their materials and work, claiming he'd definitely use them again, which he had. Twice more.

She pulled her wits about her enough to notice the stillness of the car. "Why have we stopped?"

"Because you scared me. I had to make sure you were all right."

Rubbing her forehead didn't help clear the disbelief. "I'm fine."

"Do you need some water? Or sugar?"

"Sugar?" Her confusion compounded until understanding dawned. "No. I'm not a diabetic. Let's just go."

He watched her for a few moments.

"Really, I'm okay." *Make something up.* "Brad must've mentioned the name of the company. I was surprised to hear you associated with it."

He narrowed his eyes as if trying to see into her mind. Lanelle didn't give in to the need to fidget with her hands.

"Are you sure you're okay?"

Lanelle nodded. Seemingly satisfied, Dante put the car in gear and pulled onto the road.

She let her shoulders relax as her mind processed the news. She knew next to nothing about him, but she couldn't deny that she liked him. He was successful in his own right, so if he found out she was an Astacio he wouldn't cling to her for her status or money. Or would he?

What if he and his company were involved in stealing the hospital's money? Her heart clenched at the thought of having to take down this wonderful man's reputation if he had anything to do with it. She didn't think he did, but she'd been wrong about so many other things about her project. She needed to acquire more intel. Who better to get it from than him? *It has nothing to do with liking him and wanting to press my body against his.*

With less than five minutes until they reached Peaches 'n'

Cream so Lanelle could pick up her car, she didn't have much time to interrogate him. Biting the inside of her cheek, she contemplated asking him out or letting the whole thing go.

"I have some questions about your flooring business." *I'd also like to see what this attraction pulsing between us is all about.* A deep inhale buoyed her courage. "Do you think we could get together again sometime?"

"Sure," he said, as if women asked him out on an hourly basis. "I know tomorrow is Monday, but would you like to go out to dinner?"

Time to regain control. "Do you know Chalamar's?"

"On Central Avenue? Yes."

"Let's meet there at six. I'll make a reservation."

"Or I could pick you up at your house. And drive us over."

Lanelle shook her head. If he knew where she lived, he'd have more access to her. She had to keep him at a distance. "Why, when we can drive separate cars?" She held back a wince at the lack of logic. People attempting to protect the environment would flog her for it, but she wouldn't relent.

When he pulled up next to her car in the parking lot of the restaurant, a sudden sadness filled her. "I had a great time today. Thanks."

"Me, too."

Opening the door, Lanelle reminded Dante, "Tomorrow. Six. At the restaurant." Before he had the chance to respond, she closed the door and rushed to her car.

He rolled down his window. "That will be the last time we meet anywhere. Next time I'll pick you up."

His parting comment set her heart racing. She found it endearing when a man thought his strength of will exceeded hers. She'd fight their attraction like Oscar De La Hoya in round one, but deep down she hoped to lose.

Chapter 9

A full house on a Monday evening at Chalamar's boasted of the restaurant's popularity. But everything disappeared for Lanelle except for the sight of Dante's glorious profile as the hostess led her forward.

Struggling to swallow, she gave what she hoped to be a friendly smile. When he stood and pulled out her chair, she caught a whiff of his spicy cologne. Even his scent was unique and enticing. Would he taste anything like he smelled, maybe with a hint of orange?

This is a fact-finding mission. Calm your hormones and stay focused. And yet she couldn't stop grinning.

She'd checked in with the forensic accountant this afternoon. He'd found a few discrepancies in the accounts she and her accountant had combed through but hadn't come up with anything definite. Now that Dante's company had won the bid, she hoped she could gain some insight from a contractor's angle.

The excuse made her feel better about wanting to be with him. How far could a relationship between them get? The way he spoke about his nieces and nephews, he probably wanted children of his own one day—something she couldn't provide.

She'd enjoy this last meal with him while attempting to do some sleuthing and then say goodbye to anything personal that could've blossomed, only to end in heartbreak.

"I wanted to kiss you on the cheek—" Dante rubbed his chin "—but I feared it would end with me in the hospital."

Feeling playful, Lanelle winked. "If you're man enough, you may have to try so you can find out."

"Did you issue a challenge to my masculinity?"

A hand to her chest gave her the dramatic flair she sought to convey. "Never." The air became electric as he stood and came around the table. The lingering brush of his lips on her cheek made her body burn. To stop herself from turning her head to meet his mouth with hers, she stiffened her muscles, even the ones she'd once thought she had no control over.

"I like that I get to walk away without a limp," Dante said once he'd settled in his seat.

Anything flirtatious she would've said before the kiss had flittered away. Picking up the menu, Lanelle attempted to refocus her vision.

The waitress appeared a few seconds later, sparing her from having to speak to Dante. "I'll have a frozen margarita, please."

"Sugar or salt on the rim?"

She lifted her gaze to Dante's full lips, wondering how they'd taste. "Sugar," she breathed, then cleared her throat. "I'm ready to order. I'll have the mushroom steak, medium rare, with a side of the house special mashed potatoes and the fresh vegetable medley."

The waiter veered toward Dante.

"A margarita sounds good. Only leave out everything but the tequila. Bring me the same meal as the lady."

"I'll be right back with your drinks."

"I wouldn't have pegged you for a meat-and-potatoes girl."

The comment interested her. "Really? And what did you think I'd order?"

Dante rested his elbows on the table. "Lemon shrimp scampi over angel-hair pasta."

Lanelle crinkled her nose. "I hate shrimp. But the pasta sounds good. Make it a lasagna and you would've been right on point."

"You're an enigma."

"So I've been told." She might as well find out what she wanted to know about him and his business. "How was work today?"

His congenial expression transformed into a frown as he picked up a roll and buttered it. "It didn't go as well as I'd expected."

"Why? What happened?"

His hesitation had her on the cusp of retracting the question. "Remember I told you I was doing the flooring for the new NICU wing at the hospital?"

Lanelle nodded.

"My crew and I performed a walk-through today." He shook his head. "Whoever did the construction did some shoddy work."

"What?" she screeched, then relaxed her clasped hands from their grip on the table.

"Yeah. The place looks good from a nonprofessional view, but you put anyone in there who knows even a little about building, and you'll end up with questions."

Lanelle's stomach plummeted. "Is the place safe?"

The waiter settled the drinks in front of them before Dante answered, "It's not going to collapse, but it's not the kind of quality you'd expect in a public building."

"What exactly is wrong with it?"

He angled his head. "Why are you so concerned?"

Lanelle forced herself not to reach for her drink. Nothing screamed guilt like gulping down alcohol. "It doesn't seem right that someone would build a wing for babies and have it fall on their heads. Plus, you seem to like talking about your work. If you want to change the subject, we can." *Please don't. I need to know what's wrong with my project and what to do about it.*

She picked up her drink and took a genteel sip of the slushy concoction through the straw. A little more sour than she liked it, but it could be the feeling of being in some kind of hot seat changed her taste buds. Espionage was not her forte.

"The drywall they used isn't as thick as it should've been. And the cabinetry was made of inferior core wood instead of solid wood. It's not too big a deal, considering they've laminated it."

"Will you report the issues?"

Dante downed his shot of tequila. "To whom? I'm there to do the flooring and countertops. I'm not a building inspector."

"Couldn't you mention this to the hospital administrators?" The tightness in her stomach would prevent her from eating if the conversation didn't change direction soon.

"What good would it do? They knew who they hired when they accepted the bids."

Would an uninvolved person know what he was talking about? Why take the chance? "Bids?"

"Yes. It's like a proposal, or a request to do a job." He relaxed into his seat as if settling in for a lecture. "They're supposed to be sealed, and a team from the hospital chooses which company offered the best bid. It's usually based on price. But for the hospital to choose cost and overlook the long-term quality of a product doesn't seem practical."

"Maybe they were on a tight budget."

"I doubt it. I heard Eliana Astacio contributed a lot of

money to the project. I doubt she'd want her name associated with garbage."

Lanelle's ears twitched when he mentioned her name. Before she could think of anything to say, Dante scoffed, "But you never know with people like that." He picked up another roll and broke it open.

Her back went stiff. "What do you mean?"

"You know those people. The wealthy—at least those who were born into money they didn't earn—think they're above…well, everything."

"Those people?" Should she even get into this discussion?

"I've dealt with people who fund projects such as the NICU, and believe me, up front they may seem like philanthropists tossing their money about, only to retrieve it through tax benefits. But in actuality, they're out for themselves."

Her deep breaths weren't enough to calm her. She couldn't back away from the conversation, so she slugged down half of her drink. Dredging up the most neutral voice she could muster, she said, "I take it you've met Eliana Astacio?"

"Who's ever actually met her? She keeps out of the media better than a chameleon." He shook his head. "I know her type."

More interested than annoyed in how he viewed a woman he knew very little about, she leaned forward. "Type?"

"Rich, spoiled, a debutante. She'd do anything to keep up appearances and sit in the good graces of her parents. Including break a person's heart."

Lanelle tilted her head as she studied his now sullen face, and without warning her heart melted. "Sounds like someone broke *your* heart."

His voice came out gruff. "Life happens."

Recalling all she'd been through, she nodded. "You can say that again. Who was the woman?"

He finished off his roll. "Aren't you going to try the bread? It's delicious."

Lanelle preferred to find out more about his past, but she could take a hint. Staying as far from evil carbohydrates as possible, she considered her options. As much as she hated it, she needed help with the project. Brad came to mind. He could do an inspection and let her know if the building was safe.

"Other than the shoddy workmanship—" *on my project site* "—how was your day?"

His eye contact never wavered when his voice got low and husky. "It didn't go by as quickly as I would've liked. I've been anticipating seeing you."

Her only response came as a long sip of her drink to hide the silly grin she couldn't prevent. She'd have to watch out for his charm.

Then a moment of sorrow plowed into her gut as she recalled this would be the last time they'd go out. She'd gotten the information she needed from him. Besides, why would she even think about dating someone who hated her true persona without ever having met her? Trusting a man would lead to a heartbreak she never desired to experience again.

Chapter 10

Did a blush linger under her flawless skin? He wasn't quite sure: Lanelle had seemed to be glowing from the first moment he'd met her.

Why had she been so interested in the NICU project? Even worse, she'd gotten all huffy when he'd given his opinion on Eliana Astacio. Was Lanelle involved with Eliana's brother, Miguel? He pushed away the thought as he recalled the man being a player who didn't do commitment.

Maybe he'd been a little hard on the woman. After all, he didn't know her personally, and her parents were great people. He'd learned a few things about the business world when he'd worked with her father on three of his projects. Dante had initially been awestruck after he'd read the article about the powerful Astacios in *Time* magazine.

Even if he put aside the fact that she came from money she didn't have to work for, it still remained that Eliana had built a hospital wing using cheap materials. Did she even care about the project? "I've talked enough for the night. What about you? How do you make your living?"

"I deal with investments," Lanelle said.

"What kind?"

Lanelle squirmed the slightest bit. "I like helping people start businesses with great potential, but who'd have a hard time getting financing from the bank. I loan them the money. Kind of like a micro-financier, but the interest I charge isn't anywhere as steep."

"Sounds like it takes a lot of capital on your part." Not having asked a question, he wasn't surprised by her silence. "How do you find these people?"

"Mostly word of mouth. Every once in a while, I'll discover someone by accident."

"I can't imagine all your ventures are successful."

"Like any other business, there are risks." She slid her finger down her glass, clearing a line of condensation. "I don't go in blind. I make sure the idea is good and the individual has a solid business plan and proposal."

"Do you like it?"

Her gaze remained steady. "I enjoy helping."

"You could do that any number of other ways. Putting your money in jeopardy doesn't have to be part of the plan."

She shrugged. "It's what I've been doing since after college. Seeing someone's dreams come true is one of the biggest highs I've ever experienced."

"Sounds like a great job for you."

"What about you? Do you enjoy your work?"

His head jerked back. "If Vanessa heard you ask the question, she'd laugh her ass off. I love what I do. I couldn't see myself doing anything else."

"How did you get into it?"

The waiter delivered their steaming savory plates of food. They dropped the conversation as they ate. The slight tang of the mushroom sauce set off the flavor of the beef perfectly. "Good choice," he praised.

She paused in slicing into the tender meat to look up at him. "Thanks."

Halfway through the meal, she set her cutlery down. "Tell me about your flooring business. How did you get into it?"

"It's a long story, and not all of it is interesting."

She waved her hands about. "Add some flair to the telling and I'm sure I'll be astounded."

The spurts of humor Lanelle exhibited every so often drew out a laugh from him. What would she be like if she were comfortable enough to be herself? "I don't do dramatic. But for you, I'll try. My freshman year of high school ended up being tough. Imagine me as a lanky, uncoordinated, uncool young man with a chip on his shoulder."

She perused him. "I can't."

"I'll have to show you a picture one day. Urkel from *Family Matters* had it all over me. My being dark skinned didn't help. It's amazing how cruel black kids can be to their own kind just because of skin color." He shook his head. "Anyway, I digress. My father worked as a pilot."

He waited for her reaction to that. Other than eating a forkful of mashed potatoes and looking at him with an expectation to speak, she exhibited none. Most people asked a million questions about the life of an airline pilot, even though he'd never flown a plane himself.

"He tended to bring people to the house for dinner. One day he brought this Italian man, Mr. Victor Calvano. His accent was so thick everyone in the family stopped asking him to repeat what he'd said after the fourth time. We adapted, nodding and smiling when he spoke. Not the best strategy, especially when he asked a question. It turned out he'd invited me to Italy for the summer. My dad had nodded me away."

"Was he serious?"

"Yep. When we figured out what he'd said, my dad refused the invitation."

"Understandable. Why would a stranger invite a boy to another country with him?" Lanelle scrunched her adorable nose. "Sounds suspicious and pedophile-y."

"That's not a word."

She pointed to her chest with her free hand. "In my book it is."

Dante lowered his voice. "I think I'll have to read this book one day. I'd like to see what other things you're creative about."

She didn't seem like the type of woman to roll her eyes, and yet she did it. "The story, please."

"My father thought the same thing as you until Mr. Calvano explained that he saw some kind of potential in me he'd never seen in anyone else. He thought I'd be good with his precious marble."

She arched an eyebrow. "What made him come to this conclusion?"

How come she'd had to pick up on that point? He'd hoped not to humiliate himself until at least the tenth date. "I left a minuscule detail out of the story."

Lanelle chuckled. "Must be something good. Spill it."

"I've always been into rocks. It didn't matter where I was—if I saw one that interested me, I'd take it home."

"So you had a rock collection. That's not so bad."

He shook his head. "It went beyond that. I'd spend hours in the library looking up the kind of rock. This was way before the internet got popular. I even made my parents buy me a rock-cleaning set."

Lanelle laughed. "Soap and water didn't cut it?"

"Not for me. When Mr. Calvano mentioned that he quarried marble and granite, I ran to my room and brought out two things." He shouldn't be embarrassed about the past, but being a hard-core nerd was never something he'd brag about. "My favorite rocks, all encased and labeled in a glass display I requested for Christmas one year."

"What was the second?" Her voice held a tinge of humor.

"A book I'd saved all of my allowance over six months to buy because it was so cool." He pointed to his chest with shrug. "At least I thought so. A book about quarries of the world."

Lanelle's eyes went wide. "That's a huge coincidence."

"Mr. Calvano didn't seem to think so."

"What did *you* think?"

"That he had to be out of his mind to invite me to Italy, but I sat there, intrigued. My father told Mr. Calvano he'd only let me take the journey if my parents went with us."

"He said yes?"

Dante nodded. "It turns out my potential was greater than three fully purchased trips to Italy. Until the day he died, Mr. Calvano claimed I ended up being the best investment he'd ever made. He willed the business over to me when he passed."

She narrowed her eyes. "This complete stranger gave you his company? Didn't he have any family? A child? Nieces or nephews?"

Dante struggled to stave off a wave of grief as he recalled the man he'd learned to love. "He and his wife never had children before she died about six years ago. Mr. Calvano was an only child and would speak of some distant cousins occasionally, but they weren't close. He'd mentioned the last time he saw them had been over twenty years ago."

Food seemingly forgotten, Lanelle leaned in. "And now?"

Smart woman. He'd have to keep that in mind. "When Mr. Calvano died, he willed his house in Italy and some of his money to the children of his deceased distant cousins. The business came to me with two stipulations. The first being that I maintain the name of the company."

"Which you have. What was the second?"

"I name all of my children Calvano."

Her mouth dropped open, then she reached out for her water glass and drank until it was half-empty.

"I thought it was crazy at the time, too. Now that he's gone, I'd like to immortalize him by passing his name on through my offspring. Most likely a middle name."

"What if you don't have children?"

Dante would've laughed if Lanelle wasn't staring at him as if her life depended on the answer with her fingers gripping the table. "I don't see why I wouldn't. One day I'll get married and then we'll have kids. It's the natural progression."

He could hear her swallow from where he sat. "Are you okay?"

"Yes," she croaked out before clearing her throat. "I've never heard of such a stipulation. What if your—" she paused "—wife doesn't agree to the Calvano name for her children? Especially if it's a girl."

"Of course, I'd tell her before we got married." Dante shrugged. "If she doesn't accept, then she's not the one for me."

"And if she can't have children for you?" The mumbled words had barely left her mouth before she cleared the air with a wave of her hand. "Tell me what happened with the Calvanos."

He wanted to discuss her question, but why distress her further? And yet he couldn't help wondering what had upset her. "His relatives weren't happy about the business going to an American." Dante sniffed. "A black one at that. So they sent the matter to court."

"Can't say I'm surprised."

"Neither was I, but I was disappointed. They never once came to visit this amazing man while he was alive." His voice cracked on the last word.

Lanelle reached out and clasped his hand. He let the comfort of her touch soothe him from the pain he still felt at having lost a man he'd greatly respected and loved. "Ever since the first trip to Italy, I've been his family. I know this may sound corny, but he treated me like a son."

"It's not corny at all. Life is about finding love where and when you can."

Their gazes locked as the words lingered between them. *Is she the one I never knew I wanted?*

Lanelle broke the spell encasing them by pulling her hand out of his. "So what happened with the lawsuit?"

"Mr. Calvano was a shrewd businessman. He understood the Italian system and had his lawyer write his will in a way that ensured that no one could take the company from me. He didn't count on the courts wanting to keep it in Italian hands. Even if the transition of ownership would destroy it and the legacy of the Calvano family."

Lanelle prompted, "Well?"

"The court ruled in my favor. Mostly."

"What do you mean?"

"I was ordered to pay taxes on profits for three years."

"Before or after the US deducts its taxes?" Lanelle asked.

Interesting woman. No one had ever asked him. "Before."

Her indignant anger pleased him. "How can they get away with it?"

He winced at the memory of the wrath he'd unleashed when he received the news. Tsunamis had left less destruction in their wake. It took some time, but he'd made his peace with the decision. "They also ordered five percent of the company's profits to go to the extended family." Now for the part that had perturbed Dante the most. "And to top it all off, I had to prove I could make the business expand within three years or I'd have to relinquish twenty-five percent of the company to the family."

Lanelle raised her fisted hand, and at the last second halted it from banging on the table. Her show of temper, although justified, intrigued him even further. "That's crazy. Did you appeal?"

He held up two fingers. "Twice. I hired one of the best lawyers in Italy. There'd been a precedent they'd based their decision on."

"At least they didn't threaten to take it all away."

Dante clamped down his own resurfacing anger. "They did, but Mr. Calvano's lawyer made sure the will was iron-clad so no court in the world would be able to remove me as head of the company."

Lanelle flexed her fingers, opened her mouth to speak, closed it and then unclenched her hands. "How come you aren't angrier?"

"Believe me, I was. I've had a year and a half to get over it. There's nothing I can do but comply with the court order. Mr. Calvano cautioned me something like this could happen. He advised me to stand firm. As long as the business stayed in my name, he knew I'd keep his legacy alive."

"And you have."

Dante drew his brows together. She sounded as if she knew his reputation personally. "I have a plan to get the Calvano clan off my back forever," he confided. "Once I get this PVC aspect of the company running, I know it'll be successful. I just have to make sure the hospital project is in top order so references can start pouring in." Yes, he sounded confident, but he knew he'd succeed. He'd accept nothing less.

The bid he and his team had come up with had sent him home with a headache from calculations on more than one occasion. He'd cut his profit margin drastically when he created the bid. His long-sighted vision would pay off later when he earned more clients. The goal for this project was to get his foot in the door, not to make an excessive amount of money.

Lanelle's back stiffened, and her expression became unreadable while she stared at him.

"What's wrong?"

She shook her head with a long blink. "Oh. Nothing. Your case is just the most outrageous thing I've ever heard."

"It could've been worse. No matter how much I'm forced to give away to the Italian Agency of Revenue or the Calvano clan, I'll recoup it soon enough."

"You're more positive than I'd be in your situation."

"I can't tell you how much I learned from Mr. Calvano. I owe it to him to keep his business prosperous and his name honored."

"What did he teach you?"

Dante smiled as the memories of laughter, hard work and love played through his mind. "Everything. During summer breaks, he'd take me to marble quarries all over the world, just like in my book. After the first trip, my parents didn't join us again." Dante took a moment to inhale. Telling the story of his success never got old. "He taught me about marble. From the removal of the stone from the earth straight through processing and installation. Then he drilled me about granite and limestone."

"Wow."

"I'll always be grateful to him for taking me under his wing and helping me build my confidence."

"He sounds like a wonderful man."

"He was." He cleared his throat when his voice came out husky with emotions.

The waiter's impeccable timing saved the moment. He

focused on Lanelle when he spoke. "Would you like to order dessert? Or coffee?"

"I'm fine. Thank you."

"And you, sir?"

"No, thanks. Just the bill, please." *I'd appreciate if you could convince this amazing woman to open up a little more.*

Chapter 11

If Lanelle didn't count the parts where she omitted the truth about her true identity, the fact that the man must have children at all costs and her growing suspicions of Dante, dinner had been spectacular. Something Lanelle hadn't expected.

She'd dismissed any thoughts of him doing something as underhanded as cheating the hospital in order to win the bid and grow his business. Her instincts just couldn't be that wrong about a person.

Lanelle slowed her pace, not wanting their date to end. Why let it? Since this would be the last time they'd get together, she might as well relish it. After his revelation of needing to have a child, she knew she wasn't the one for him. She'd never give him what he desired. Admitting it to herself didn't make her feel any better about letting him go.

The cool night air raised goose bumps on her arms and sent a shiver coursing through her.

"You're cold." Dante removed his suit jacket and draped it over her shoulders.

The allure of his scent encapsulated her. *Maybe he'll forget to take it back. And I'll sniff it all night like some kind of loser? Not a good idea.* She knew she wouldn't offer the coat back once they got to her car. "Thanks for the jacket and paying for dinner. You didn't—"

"I wanted to, so I did. Arguing about it when the check came didn't make things easy on me."

"It's my way."

He nudged her with a strong shoulder. "So I've noticed. Just the tiniest bit stubborn."

She thrust her chin up. "No, I'm tenacious."

"Sure you are."

She laughed. As they reached her car, she thought to ask him for another date. What would be the point? *To live a little instead of rolling up into a protective ball of loneliness.* At a loss for words, she unlocked her car.

"Lanelle?"

She tilted her face up to peer into his eyes. "Yes?"

"It's not my style to ask, but it seems safer this way."

Now he had her curious. "What does?"

"Can I kiss you?"

The air rushed out of her lungs. For the past couple of hours she'd hoped for it but hadn't expected one. What would it mean? Taking this risk would be a big leap of faith for her. She only wished she could accept it without getting hurt.

Lanelle took forever to answer Dante's question. When she opened her mouth, he thought for sure she'd tell him no. He should've leaned in and stolen the kiss. And yet he couldn't. He had too much respect for her wishes to go against them. The fear of her self-defense skills didn't come into consideration. He flexed his pinkie. At least not too much.

"I'd like that."

Had he heard her right? Her dark expectant eyes told him he had. The burden of an extraordinary first kiss pressed down on his shoulders. *Relax and kiss her before she gets into her car and drives away. If it's bad, it's bad.*

Slowly, so as not to frighten her, Dante stepped a little closer and raised his hands to frame her face. Her breaths came out shallow as her lids lowered. Confidence returned as he leaned in and brushed the lightest kiss he could manage across her lips. *So sweet.* He repeated the action. When she reached out, grabbed his shoulders and responded by kissing him back, he lost the need to keep the kiss tender.

His tongue dashed out to savor the fullness of her lower lip. When she opened her mouth on a moan, he delved in. Along with her scent of roses, the smell of his cologne on her heightened his senses to astonishing levels. Everything about her was glorious, including the taste of mint on her tongue. She molded her body against him. Winding her arms around his neck, the jacket slipped away as she kissed him back with a fierce hunger.

Rather than make love to her against her car in a public parking lot, he eased back until he felt steady enough to finish how he'd started it: with a perfect caress that had her shifting forward when he released her lips.

Stroking her cheek with the back of his fingers as he watched her eyes flutter open, he stepped away from the temptation she presented.

What did someone say after such a mind-blowing experience? *Ask her for another date.* His mouth refused to cooperate with the order from his brain. He stared into the depths of her eyes, willing himself not to kiss her again.

A flick of her tongue to lick her lips almost crumbled his resolve. He sent up a prayer that Vanessa's powers of persuasion would work on Lanelle. She'd come up with the idea to invite Lanelle to Italy with them as her guest. He hadn't vetoed it, but he doubted the woman would relent and take the journey. But right then he wanted nothing more than to have her by his side in the most beautiful country in the world.

He picked up his jacket from the ground. *I'll see her on the flight to Italy*, he promised himself. Out loud he said, "Get in the car so I can make sure you're safe."

She snapped out of her daze. "I can take care of myself."

And the spitfire is back. "Please?" The one word induced the slightest grin. He'd have to say it more often if it made her so happy.

Opening the door, she slid into her seat. After turning on the engine, she waved as she drove away.

Although sure he'd done the right thing by letting her go, he still regretted not having her in his arms. Vanessa had better deliver on enticing Lanelle to say yes to the trip.

Daydreaming about Dante and the amazing things his lips had done to her wouldn't help Lanelle get through the proposal she should've finished reading at least three times in the last two hours. It would help if the business plan made sense. How could a person make money from opening a restaurant that served only protein? The Atkins craze had come and gone.

Although she hadn't been completely up front with Dante last night, at least she could claim having told the truth. She'd kept her wealth and family name a secret. *He doesn't need to know everything about me.* Then why did she have niggling guilt?

She had known it was her destiny to help people ever since she was young. The best way she'd learned to do it was by sharing the money she'd been born into. Lanelle possessed an uncanny intuition when it came to discerning who needed her assistance and those people who attempted to scam her. Her parents' support over the years prodded her on.

She had soon learned the truth of the old adage that giving more away meant she'd receive more, which happened in spades. Sometimes the money poured in from the most unexpected places.

Lanelle closed the proposal's much-too-thin folder and scooted back from the glass surface of her home office desk. A quick glance at the clock told her she had about an hour before her lunch with Toshia.

She'd spoken to the chief administrator of the hospital earlier to ask about the clearance she'd requested last week to assess all the bids that had come in for the project. She hadn't told the board that she'd hired a specialist to help her find the truth about the missing money. The administrator said he hadn't received permission from the board to release the records. Her instincts had gone on an even higher alert. With forced patience she'd asked him to do his best to get her access to the bids.

Her second call of the day had been to Bradley, requesting him to do a brief walk-through of the current structure to see if it was safe.

Unfortunately, he'd be out of town for a couple of weeks. When he offered one of his workers, Lanelle had refused. She'd have to wait because he was the only one she trusted for the task. Dante had mentioned the place wasn't crumbling down around their heads. By the time Brad did the inspection, she'd have learned where the money had disappeared. If more work needed to be done, they'd retrieve at least some of the cash from the one responsible for taking the money and use it to reconstruct.

Her ringtone, Vivaldi's "Spring," stopped her in the midst of standing up for a full-body stretch. "Hi, Vanessa."

"Hey, Lanelle." Not one to waste words, Vanessa got to the point. "Do you have time to meet with me today? I want to ask you a question."

On her guard, Lanelle picked up a pen and tapped it

against the proposal. "Whatever it is, you can ask over the phone."

"Not this one. I need to see your reaction."

Oh, dear. Lanelle's stomach churned at the possibility of the questions the girl could've come up with. Anything from advice about clothes to, God forbid, her uncle. "I'm meeting my best friend for lunch. Would you like to join us?"

A lengthy pause came from the other end. "Vanessa? Are you still there?"

"I don't want to intrude or anything."

"It's no problem. Toshia won't mind. I have to warn you she says what's on her mind, but I think she'll tone it down with you around. In fact, I insist you come with us. Maybe we'll have a normal conversation for once."

"I don't know."

The more Lanelle thought about it, the better it sounded. Toshia wouldn't harass her about her date with Dante if Vanessa were there. "I insist. Do you have classes this afternoon?"

"Nope. They've ended, and we're starting finals next week."

"That's perfect. I'll come get you. Are you home or at school?"

"On campus."

Not giving Vanessa a chance to back out, she sealed the arrangement. "The usual place in thirty minutes."

"Sure."

"You can try to sound a little more enthusiastic. It'll be fun. I'll see you soon."

"Bye."

Lanelle sighed, concerned about the young woman. Getting to know Vanessa had set her maternal instincts ablaze. She'd thought they'd been buried with her twins.

Lanelle would've made such a wonderful mother, stern, fun and undoubtedly loving.

She pushed the thoughts away but they bounced back to the forefront. *Who says you can't have children? The benefit of raising a new life would far outweigh the risks, and if you chose an Rh-negative man, the baby wouldn't have to fight for his or her life in the womb. Or you could adopt.*

For the first time in years she was able to consider the potential of having children without breaking into a cold sweat. What had changed?

Dante's earnest face flashed into her mind and she shook the image away, along with her musings about having a family.

Chapter 12

Vanessa worried her lower lip while they sat in a booth waiting for Toshia. "Are you sure she won't mind my joining you?"

Lanelle reassured her for the fifth time. "Yes. And stop chewing your lip."

"Nervous habit."

"There's nothing to be anxious about." Lanelle assessed Vanessa. "Wearing lipstick helped me to break the habit. I don't know much about the youth of today, but I would've thought someone as beautiful as you would want to enhance your features. How come you don't wear makeup?"

"I used to. When I got sick, I stopped." She hitched a shoulder and glided a hand over her intricately designed cornrows, which ended in a ponytail. "I guess I never felt pretty enough to start again."

"What are you talking about? You're gorgeous, inside and out." Her heart hurt for Vanessa. She'd lost so much to cancer. The least she could do was boost her confidence a little. Lanelle reached into her purse and pulled out three Sephora tubes of lipstick. Choosing a pale red color, she opened it and wiped it on a paper napkin. "You don't need it, but try this. It'll look pretty on you."

Vanessa scrunched her nose. "It's red. Besides, you're so much lighter than me it probably won't look good."

"You have a similar complexion as Toshia. We bought the exact same color. I know it'll look good on you." Lanelle handed her a compact mirror. "Try it on."

Vanessa smeared the color on her lips. Turning her head from side to side, she finally smiled. "It looks good." She then proceeded to open her purse and drop it in. "Thanks."

Lanelle held out her hand. "Oh, no, you don't. Give it back."

Vanessa pouted as she pulled the tube out and gave it to Lanelle.

"If you behave, I may take you shopping. How's a week from Saturday?"

"Can't. We're leaving for Italy that day."

She'd completely forgotten. "How exciting. I wish I was going. Who did you decide to take as your guest?"

Toshia strolled up to the table and sat on the side of the booth next to Vanessa. If the young woman hadn't been so fast, she would've been Toshia's cushion. "Who's this?"

"No 'hello'? 'Sorry I'm late'? Nothing but rudeness," Lanelle said.

Toshia raised her lips into a smile for half a second. "Howdy. Kindly introduce us. Is that better?"

Lanelle shook her head, expecting nothing different. "This is my friend Vanessa Peters. Vanessa, this is Toshia Covington."

Toshia extended a hand to Vanessa, and they shook. "Nice to meet you, Vanessa. See, I can be well mannered. I just need to be inspired."

"Why are you late?"

"I'm the one who should be asking questions. How was your date with Mr. Tall, Dark and Afro last night?"

Vanessa leaned forward with her elbows propped on the table.

"I don't think I mentioned that Vanessa is Dante's niece."

Toshia turned to the girl. "I can see the resemblance. You have the same spectacular light brown eyes. Now tell me what happened. Unless it's too juicy to spill in front of a minor."

Vanessa threw her shoulders back. "I'll be twenty-one next week."

"Good for you, sweetie. You're still a baby, but now I know you can handle the details."

Both women stared at Lanelle.

How come she'd forgotten how news-hungry Toshia could get? The waiter came to their table, relieving her of the need to answer. After putting in their orders, the two went at it again.

Vanessa batted her lashes. "I think Lanelle is quiet because she had *too* good of a time with my uncle."

Toshia raised her brows. "You'd better talk, and do it fast. I want every detail of what happened last night. Don't think I didn't notice how you swayed on the dance floor with him. I couldn't tell the two of you apart."

It was Vanessa's turn for her eyes to go wide. "I once overheard a woman say that Uncle D dances like he's making love. I know I shouldn't be asking, but is it true? Does he?"

Toshia bobbed her head. "Yeah, does he?"

Lanelle tried one last time to escape the double harassment. She waved a finger between Vanessa and Toshia. "What the hell's going on here between you two?"

"That's not the question on deck, my evasive friend," Toshia said. "What we need to know is what's happening between you and Dante. Everything else is irrelevant." Toshia held up a hand, and Vanessa reciprocated with a high five.

"First of all, we've never come close to making love,

so I can't answer your question, Vanessa." But after the dance and the kiss, she'd guess the answer to be a resounding yes. "Not that I would tell you if we had. We ate dinner last night at Chalamar's, had a good time and then went home."

Toshia wiggled her eyebrows. "Together?"

"No."

"What do you think, Vanessa? Is she telling the truth?"

Vanessa shrugged and turned to Toshia. "I don't see why she'd lie. Especially to you. You seem like you'd be able to wear her down."

"I like your new little friend, Lanelle. She's smart."

"More like a smart-ass," Lanelle mumbled.

Vanessa tapped a short-nailed finger on the table. "I heard that."

"Good." Lanelle created space on the table so the waiter could place her beef burrito down. The aromatic spices from Vanessa's quesadilla and Toshia's taco salad made her mouth water. After a few bites of the burrito, Lanelle asked Vanessa, "What did you want to ask me that you couldn't over the phone?"

Vanessa placed the cheese-laden food on the plate as she finished chewing. She threw a furtive glance at Toshia and seemed to make up her mind. "Can you come to Italy with us?"

Lanelle should've known better than to have food in her mouth when the girl spoke. Swallowing the wrong way, she coughed until she had tears in her eyes. Toshia rushed to her side and banged on her back, making things worse. Lanelle pushed her friend away, rasping out, "Stop hitting me." Reaching for the water, she took a sip, then continued to cough.

"Save a woman's life and she yells at you. Some people are just ungrateful."

Gritting her teeth, Lanelle took deep breaths to replace the oxygen she'd lost for those few seconds. "Thank you."

"That's more like it."

Lanelle focused her gaze on Vanessa. "What happened to taking one of your friends?"

"You're my friend. Besides, everyone has plans. Uncle D said Keith could come, but he's going to be working on his aunt's vineyard in California for the summer."

Lanelle quirked a brow. "Dante relented?"

Toshia broke a piece of the taco-shell bowl. "What are you two talking about?"

"My uncle is taking the family to Italy for my birthday. He said I could have a guest."

"And you want Lanelle to go with you?"

Vanessa nodded.

"I approve," Toshia said. "I've been trying to make her take a vacation for the past year."

Toshia didn't play fair. "Things have been hectic."

"Look at you, you're so exhausted you're choking on burritos. Lord knows what'll happen next. You need some fun and rest. You've always wanted to travel to Italy, so go."

Try as she might, Lanelle couldn't ignore Toshia's valid points. "What about Dante?"

"What about him?" Toshia intercepted. "Didn't I say you should have some fun while you're there? Vanessa, cover your ears for a moment."

She did as she was told.

Toshia leaned across the table. "You haven't liked a guy in forever. Why are you holding back? You have to leave the past behind at some point."

"But…"

"No. You're going to Italy, and that's all there is to it. As soon as we leave here, we're going shopping."

Vanessa looked between the two women.

How could she argue with her best friend? The woman oftentimes knew what she needed before she did. Lanelle could do without her gloating about it, though. One last try. "You know I'm trying to figure out what's going on with the NICU and—"

"Isn't that accounting expert working on it? The project can survive for a week without you."

Lanelle held up her index and middle fingers. "Two weeks."

"Whatever. If something shady is going on, you'll dig it out after a wonderful vacation. I'm sure your mind will be sharper then, too. Better able to solve mysteries. You're going."

Lanelle's stomach fluttered with excitement. "I know you can hear us, and you look ridiculous. Uncover your ears."

Vanessa grinned. "So you'll come with us?"

Against her better judgment and under Toshia's glare, Lanelle said, "Yes."

Vanessa raised a fist to Toshia's and bumped. "Thanks, Toshia. That was easier than I thought. I was ready to play the remission card."

Lanelle knew it would've worked just as well as Toshia's bulldozing. She froze as her heart beat triple time. How would she survive fourteen days with Dante? Even now, the thought of repeating those kisses made her lips tingle. How could she resist him when he'd be in close proximity all the time?

And according to him, Italy ranked as the most romantic place in the world. Lanelle took a piece of ice from her glass and crunched it. *What have I done?*

Chapter 13

Manny Cooper wiped the sweat from his forehead with an already drenched shirt. "What's riding you, man?"

Dante stopped midserve and stared at the only friend he'd kept in contact with from junior high. "Nothing." He tossed the blue squash ball up and swung his racket, smashing the sphere into the wall. Manny sprinted to the side, hitting it with his signature light touch.

Anticipating the move, Dante lunged forward and slammed the ball against the front wall, sending it ricocheting backward and making Manny backtrack for it. Quick as lightning, he got it just in time to lob it into the air before touching the wall.

Dante smiled and hit the ball with such a practiced gentle hand he could've sworn it moved in slow motion. Manny wasn't one to give up easily, and he dived for the ball, reaching it just before it hit the ground a second time.

The rebound headed straight for Dante. He put all his strength into creating the winning shot. A groan of pain rent through the air when the ball careened into Manny's ass.

"That's the second damn time you've hit me today. First with your racket and now this."

"Sorry, man."

Manny rubbed his behind with a wince. "The smile you're sporting isn't giving me the impression of a true apology."

Dante raised his arm, clearing off both sweat and the smile on his soaked T-shirt. "Are you okay?"

"You know it didn't cause permanent damage, but what's wrong with you?"

Moving to pick up the ball, Dante avoided eye contact. He should be at his office getting ready for the trip to Italy by clearing off his huge to-do list. Unbeknownst to Vanessa, it wouldn't be a true vacation for him. He had a meeting scheduled while there.

Had Lanelle accepted the offer to go with them?

He'd put money on it she'd declined. Why would she want to spend time with a family she barely knew and a man who obviously disturbed her peace of mind?

Frustrated, Dante had no idea how to proceed with her. "I met this woman." He shifted on his feet to keep his muscles warm. He had more game left in him.

"You mean someone you can date, or someone you'll screw around with?" Manny had married right after college and tended to plot ways to get Dante to join the fold. "Wait, don't tell me you're actually considering her for a relationship. Holy hell. Has the world turned inside out?"

"Don't be ridiculous. I just want to get to know her better." Deciding they wouldn't play anymore, Dante bent at the hips and stretched his hamstrings.

Manny did the same. "I've only heard you say it once before. Now I *know* it's serious. What's the issue?"

Dante switched positions to stretch his calf and attempted to keep the conversation off the only woman he'd ever been serious about before—and who'd ground his heart in a blender. "I feel like she's hiding something."

"If you haven't learned by now, I'll clue you in. All women are hiding something."

"Very funny."

Manny chuckled. "I wasn't joking. What gives you the impression she's holding out information?"

As they sat on the wooden floor stretching, Dante gave the watered-down version of what happened at the fund-raiser and the times they'd gone out.

Manny shook his head. "Circumstantial at best, man. I'm talking all of it. There's only one thing you can do."

Dante perked up. "What?"

"If you care about her, then ask her what she's hiding."

His snort echoed through the room. "She'd only lie."

"Or she'd explain everything. Don't let Martha's duplicity keep you away from a worthy female."

At the mention of his ex-fiancée, Dante growled. He'd loved the woman to the extent that she'd soured him on relationships when he found out she'd dumped him for someone of her own social status. She'd claimed his heart from the first moment he'd seen her. Neither of them cared that she came from money and him from a middle-class home. They'd dated for their last two years of college. During their senior year when he'd proposed, she said yes. But when he'd asked to visit her at home, she always found an excuse.

During the last few days of school, Martha told him they wouldn't be getting married because she was engaged to someone her parents had set her up with. Someone who could take care of her in the manner she'd become accustomed to.

Ever since that devastating experience, he preferred to keep his relationships light enough to never let commitment see the light of day. Dante picked up his racket and jumped up. "Whatever, man. Thanks for the game."

"Ask her and see what she says," Manny insisted as they headed toward the locker room.

Dante retrieved his phone from the locker where he'd stored his gear and sent his niece a text. Is Lanelle coming with us?

Before he'd stripped down for the showers, Vanessa's one-word message came through. YES!

Elated, Dante schemed. He had two weeks to get Lanelle to at least like him. Where better to do it than the most romantic country in the world? The trip to Italy would be perfect. Bless Vanessa's nosy, interceding heart for suggesting that Lanelle come along with them on her chosen birthday gift.

He'd been sure Lanelle would say no, especially considering he'd be paying for it. But the woman had a soft spot for Vanessa, and his manipulative niece had probably played on it.

He needed lessons from the girl.

After their date, he'd called Lanelle to make sure she'd gotten home without incident. A person would get the impression they were complete strangers from the icy tone she'd given him. It had him second-guessing what had happened not even thirty minutes before when she'd been hot enough to burn him while in his arms.

What did Lanelle need in a man that he didn't possess? The much too short dinner they'd shared had cinched him. He had liked everything about her, from her poise to the boisterous laughter she wasn't ashamed of expressing. Unlike with Martha, who had betrayed him without an inkling of warning, the idea of Lanelle keeping a secret disturbed him.

Dante had stopped for Chinese food before heading back to work for another late night. He rotated to look out the huge glass-paned window of his office. The city of Cleveland sprawled below his twenty-story view with buildings lighting up the night. He'd chosen the metropolis as his home base in order to be close to his family.

The business required a lot of traveling to install quality marble and granite all over the world. Pride swelled at his ability to maintain the outstanding reputation initiated by Mr. Calvano's great-grandfather.

Sometimes, like now, he'd sit in amazement, not understanding how it had all come to be his. In high school, as soon as he touched the marble still stuck within the earth, he'd fallen in love.

Until Lanelle, he'd never felt such a fire in his gut for anything but his family and marble. The fascination he'd held for rocks since his childhood had made him a perfect fit for the business. The raw beauty of the stone still attached to the earth had enthralled him when he'd first visited a quarry. He had spent hours watching them extract large blocks of marble.

To this day, each time he saw the marble being cut into the slabs that they'd use to create their countertop and flooring masterpieces, a chill raced through him. His heart would swell with pride once the installation project was completed. There was nothing as satisfying than smoothing his hands over the piece of stone he'd helped to install for people to appreciate.

It wasn't until he first touched Lanelle's hand that he'd felt the same sense of joyous wonder. Without warning, over a tiny struggle to obtain a piece of cake, he'd fallen in love with the woman.

The exquisite stone had loved him back unconditionally. There were no emotional expectations with marble the way there were with women. Would Lanelle ever feel the same about him?

Finishing the report to his executives so his business wouldn't collapse while he was away should've been top

Chapter 14

The luxurious antique-style hotel room, with its heavy dark furniture and thick brocade drapes, reminded Lanelle of the trips she'd taken to other European countries with her parents when on break from school. Why hadn't she ever traveled to Italy? Her parents had been here on numerous occasions. From what she'd seen so far, Dante had been right about its magnificence in both landscape and architecture.

Lanelle knocked on the door adjoining her room with Vanessa's.

"Come in."

When Lanelle opened the door, Vanessa's small frame lay on the bed. Poor thing must have been exhausted after the long flight.

"Are you okay, CocoVan?"

Vanessa sat upright. "Please, stop calling me that."

Ever since she'd heard the reason why Dante use it, she'd enjoyed torturing her with the nickname. "Why?"

"Because I hate it."

"Then why do you smile before you scowl? Yeah, I see it every time your uncle says it. How are you feeling?"

"I'm ready to roam the streets of Venice and maybe

buy a cute sundress or two. With some matching strappy sandals." Lanelle's stomach rumbled. They giggled. "How could you be hungry after all the food they served us on the plane?"

"We ate about four hours ago," Lanelle said. "More than enough time for my ridiculously fast metabolism to digest it. I'll grab my bag and we'll get the others. What do you think of Venice so far?"

"So cool. The water taxi was the best. The buildings are really old, but beautiful." Vanessa's hands gestured wildly. "I can't wait to see the rest of the city. The one place I really want to go is Saint Mark's Basilica. The way Uncle D talks about the marble made me curious. I wonder if he's ever been inside the building or he's only read about it when he went to college."

"Knowing his appreciation for the stone, he probably spent days there not sleeping or eating. Just caressing the marble."

Vanessa clapped and kicked her feet in the air with her laughter. "I know, right? This is Italy, the land of marble. We're in some deep trouble."

"What else do you want to see while we're here?"

"The Peggy Guggenheim Collection would be nice, but it's okay if we don't get to it. I could sit and watch the hot guys all day. Did you see them?"

How could she not? At every turn, a cutie stood in her face. From the water taxi driver to the handsome, light brown-eyed man who'd sat on her left-hand side. She'd been inundated with eye candy. "They were okay."

"Did you have your eyes closed the whole time?"

"No. The gorgeous architecture kept my attention." Lanelle paused. "Um…okay. There were some fine men around." *None of them compared to your uncle.*

"Now you sound normal."

"Let's go. I'm looking forward to tasting some authentic Italian cuisine. I brought a couple of my Thanksgiving Day pants. You know, the ones with the elastic waist. You all might have to roll me out of this country." Lanelle distended her flat stomach so it paunched out.

Vanessa slid off the raised bed. "Right behind you."

The colors, scents and sights of Italy had completely morphed for Dante. He'd never enjoyed the land more. He'd been born and raised in the United States and loved it, but there was something about Italy and its richly steeped culture that drew him back time and time again. Even when one of his executives could make the trip, he'd always come. If he didn't find it so important to be with his family, he'd make Italy his home base.

And now the opportunity had presented itself to share his world with people he loved. Including Lanelle, who sat across the table eating strawberry gelato as she listened with intent to whatever his sister blabbed on about.

Dante's heart thudded a little faster when he looked at her. He still couldn't believe she was with him. She'd stuck to Vanessa like glue, seeming to avoid him for the past three days. Attempts to spend a little secluded time with her on one of the gondola rides in Venice had proved fruitless.

Legend said that if a couple kissed on a gondola under the Bridge of Sighs at sunset when the bells of St. Mark's tolled, they'd be granted eternal love and happiness. He'd never wanted a legend to be truer, but Lanelle had refused to go with him. He wondered if she knew about the story.

No matter how hard Vanessa tried to make it happen, not using subtle methods by anyone's stretch of imagination, Lanelle refused to be alone with him.

There had to be an explanation. He sensed she liked him more than she wanted to admit. He'd caught her staring in his direction a few times with desire blazing in her eyes. Before he could address it, the blankness had returned.

What had her so terrified? It couldn't be him.

Vanessa's comment drew his attention. "Can we leave Ryan here tomorrow when we go to Carrara? He can be so embarrassing." She cut her gaze to her little brother licking a drop of his melting rainbow gelato from his arm.

"Do we have to go to another museum? They're boring." The boy frowned. "And you can't touch anything. Isn't there a place with rides and fun stuff?"

Dante handed Ryan a napkin. "Didn't you have fun on the gondolas?"

"Huh?"

"Say 'pardon me,'" Cynthia instructed.

"Pardon me?"

Being a parent never stopped. Dante took a quick look at Lanelle. The slight downward tilt of her lips as she watched Ryan changed when she looked up to meet his eyes. What had made her seem so sad all of a sudden?

Vanessa sniggered. "The boat ride where you almost fell in."

Cynthia's glare dared the girl to laugh. "And whose fault was that? You were supposed to be watching him. Instead, you had your eyes on the group of young men coming in the opposite direction."

Alan chuckled. "At least Lanelle caught him before he ended up in the water."

Ryan scraped the last spoonful of gelato from his bowl. "I wanted to see if there were fish in it."

Dante dug up another enjoyable moment for Ryan. "You seemed to like the train ride from Venice to Milan."

Vanessa laughed. "He had his face pressed against the window the whole time." She pinched her brother's cheek and, using a voice normally reserved for babies, said, "You were so adorable."

Ryan pushed her hand away. "Mom, Vanessa's bothering me."

"Leave your brother alone."

"I have a feeling Rome is the city you'll enjoy most," Dante reassured.

"I think I would've enjoyed Milan more if we'd come during Fashion Week." Vanessa held up her index finger and her thumb with a space between. "I can't believe we missed it by a month."

Cynthia nodded with enthusiasm. "It would've been nice to see a live fashion show in Milan. My friends would've been so jealous."

"You sound like your daughter," Alan said.

Cynthia straightened her shoulders. "She had to get it from somewhere."

"Uncle D?"

Dante should know better than to answer Vanessa when her voice got syrupy. "Yes?"

"Do you think we can come back in—"

"No." Dante shut down the request and turned his attention from his pouting niece back to his nephew. "I think you'll like Rome. We'll make sure you're well entertained there."

Ryan's eyes lit up. "With rides?"

A sudden idea of how he could spend more alone time with Lanelle hit him, and he smiled as if he was a five-year-old on Christmas Day. "We'll see what we can do. I guarantee you'll have a great time." To be young again without a worry in the world other than ensuring no one stole his joy. Dante pretended to look bored. "I'm pretty sure you won't be asking about rides anymore once you get on a helicopter tomorrow."

A wide grin split Ryan's face when the information registered. "Really?"

"For the rest of the time we're here—" Dante paused

for a bit of dramatic effect "—we'll travel by helicopter. There's too much to see to spend so much time on the road."

He winked at Lanelle. She didn't hide her amusement before looking out into the street.

Vanessa relinquished her small tantrum over not returning during Fashion Week. "This is the best birthday present ever. Thank you."

He'd do anything within his power for his family. "You're welcome. Tomorrow we're heading to my favorite city in all of Italy."

"What makes it your favorite?" Ryan asked.

"The finest marble that ever existed comes from there." Vanessa mimicked Dante.

"I'm glad you've been paying attention to my little lessons, CocoVan."

Dante caught Vanessa's eye and, in a casual manner, tugged at his ear. That was their prearranged gesture to get him and Lanelle alone for the first time during the trip. He'd made a commitment to open her eyes to how good they could be together, and by any means necessary he'd see it happen. This meant recruiting Vanessa's help.

Strolling through the gorgeous streets of Milan with Lanelle would surely infuse a little romance into her. She'd been more relaxed on this trip than the few times they'd met. He tugged his ear again when Vanessa didn't pick up their signal.

Vanessa stood. "Anybody up for a walk?"

"I'm exhausted," Cynthia admitted. "Today was a busy day. Ryan looks like he's about to fall out."

Alan grabbed his youngest child's hand. "We'll head back to the hotel."

As expected, Lanelle moved to Vanessa's side. "I'll go."

They waited as Dante settled the bill. "I'm ready." They strolled past the hotel, ostensibly to drop off the nonwalkers. A few feet after saying good-night to her parents and brother, Vanessa yawned, her mouth wide enough to extend beyond the fingers covering it. The girl had a flair for the overdramatic. "Fatigue just hit me. I'm going up to my room. You two go on ahead." She turned and trotted back to the hotel before Lanelle could say a word.

"She's such a faker," Lanelle muttered.

He tampered down a smile. "What did you say?"

"I've been set up." Hands on hips, she looked him in the eyes. "You never play with your ear."

Had she been watching him that closely? A tremor of excitement raced down his spine. *Keep it casual.* "Milan at night awaits to be seen. Do you still want to go?"

She regarded him. "Only if you cease and desist scheming with your niece."

"Will you promise not to avoid me for the rest of the trip?" He knew he had her when she bent her head.

"I wasn't avoiding you."

With no response to the denial, he started down the sidewalk, happy she'd joined him.

Halfway down the block, Lanelle spoke. "I can see why you love Italy so much. It's beautiful. Thank you once again for this gift."

"I'm glad you're having a good time, but you can thank Vanessa. She's the one who invited you."

"But she didn't pay for it." Arching an eyebrow, the sexy smirk appeared. "Unless she did?"

"One day Vanessa will be able to take us around the world from her pocket, but for now she can barely afford a sandwich from the deli."

An unexpected tinkle of laughter came from Lanelle. "I know what you mean. I can see the potential ready to burst from her. If only she knew what she wanted to do with her life, she could focus and blow us all out of the water with her greatness."

"She's special."

They walked along the uncrowded streets at a leisurely pace before he said, "I'd like to hold your hand. Will you let me?"

She hesitated a few seconds before turning her palm upward. "When in Rome, right?" She gestured to the few couples passing by holding hands and locked in each other's arms.

He laced their fingers, getting accustomed to the heat pulsing into him. "Rome is in a couple of days. You might want to consider waiting to use the statement until we get there."

"I'll keep it in mind."

Chapter 15

If Lanelle didn't get a hold of herself, she'd soon ask Dante to kiss her on the bridge. *Damn subliminal messages. Don't these people know public displays of affection are frowned upon for a reason?*

Handholding was new to her. Doing it in Italy had manifested into a fantasy she never knew she'd had. What would it be like to confide in him? To fold into his sexual aura? She'd been pulled in kicking and screaming, but she couldn't resist for too much longer.

Maybe Italy had the same reputation as Vegas, where whatever happened stayed in the midst of these buildings wedged against each other.

"Before you, I'd never walked holding someone's hand," she admitted.

He jerked his head back. "Really?"

"At least not as an adult."

"No boyfriend lured you into it?"

"I went to a girls' boarding school, so I didn't get many opportunities to be around guys. And when I got married… let's just say my husband wasn't the affectionate sort."

A hitch in his step pulled her to a stop just as he let go of her. "Are you married?"

Lanelle blinked, realizing she'd forgotten an important prefix when she'd mentioned Conrad. "Divorced. I should've called him my ex-husband."

"Oh."

She continued forward when he did, but he didn't grab her hand. The need to tell him everything pulled at her. *Why should I? It's none of his business.* Maybe if he knew about her deficiencies, he'd back off and stop pursuing her. Lanelle gave him a sidelong glance. He didn't seem the type to step away from anything he felt passionate about. Her knees weakened for the briefest of moments, knowing he'd decided to focus his attention on her.

He pointed to the left. "There's a café. Would you like to have a drink?"

"I'd rather keep strolling." She liked the way he didn't harass her for more information about her past.

Pressing a hand to her lower abdomen, she took the plunge after a few minutes of silence. "I was married for three years."

Dante turned to her. "Listen, you don't have to go down this road. If you don't want to get involved with me because you're still in love with your ex, then that's fine."

"What?" Then she laughed. It sounded a little hysterical to her own ears, but she couldn't help it. "How the hell did you deduce that?"

Dante backed away a step. "Isn't it what you've been hiding from me?"

Lanelle sobered in an instant. How could he tell she hadn't been forthright with him? Obviously, he'd come to the most preposterous conclusion a person could make. "What makes you think I've been hiding something from you?"

"It took many years and mistakes, but I've learned how to read people." His gaze refused to release her, seeming to probe into the depths of her mind. "I got the impression you were trying to throw me off your track by averting some of my questions."

Time to do it again. "I'm not in love with my ex-husband."

He waved a hand between them. "Then what's the issue with us? I like you, and I know you're attracted to me. But from the beginning you've been fighting it."

Feeling like some kind of cliché, standing in the middle of the street pouring out her feelings, Lanelle continued walking. He needed to know the truth about the woman he claimed to like so he could back away before he became emotionally invested.

She crossed her arms over her chest, rubbing her hands along her arms. She looked up at his profile. "I met Conrad while getting my MBA."

His raised eyebrows told her more than any comment he could've made.

"I'm not just a pretty face."

"Beautiful."

"What?"

He reached out and stroked her cheek with the back of his fingers, leaving a heated trail with his touch. "I never thought you were just a *beautiful* face."

She cleared her throat. "Thank you."

A few steps later, Dante prompted, "What happened after you met him?"

Unlike the turmoil of desire Dante wrought, her relationship with Conrad had basically been platonic. "We became friends when we were partnered for a project in a shared class. It took him a year to ask me out, and when he did I was surprised. We didn't roll like that. I saw him as a friend and thought he did, too.

"When he broke it all down, it made perfect sense. We came from similar backgrounds and were good friends. I'd always heard a good relationship was built on friendship." *Bunch of liars.*

Dante reached for her hand and brought it to his lips. "What about passion?"

Her stomach flipped at the intimacy of his tone and touch. "It would've been nice, but to be honest, it wasn't what I was searching for."

He let their joined hands drop between them as he held on, his mood having seemed to lighten. "Which was?"

"Stability and a family. I love my parents, but when I was a child they traveled a lot. Even now, they spend more time in the air than they do in their home." Lanelle sighed, wishing she'd had a more consistent childhood. What would be the point of a privileged woman complaining about something she could never change?

"So who raised you?"

"I attended boarding school. From first grade straight through high school, I went to the best. On breaks, my brothers and I would join Mom and Dad on whatever adventure they'd decided to take. Things were even better if we were in the house as a family."

He angled himself to look at her. "Did you find it lonely?"

"A little." Lanelle shrugged. "I didn't know any differently until I got to high school and some of the students weren't boarders. I learned some of the kids actually lived with their families all the time. I realized my parents loved me, but they didn't really want me around."

"That can't be true."

She shook her head. "Of course it wasn't, but I didn't learn the truth until later in life. They loved me and my brothers, but some people aren't meant to take care of their kids on a full-time basis. I figured when I got married and had children, I'd have them with me constantly to make sure they knew they were loved." Lanelle's heart constricted with the lost opportunities.

"Let me guess. Your ex never traveled."

Conrad had frustrated her with his lack of adventure. Whenever she'd suggest a vacation destination, he'd find some excuse not to go. "You got it. He'd lived his whole life in Boston, and he hated change. He was the most predictable person I'd ever dated."

"You mean boring."

She pointed her free finger at him. "Don't tell him I told you, but yes."

Dante's expression fell. "And you still married him? You don't seem like the type of woman who'd like living a static life. Weren't you the one who suggested we go hang gliding? When everyone but Ryan shot it down, you wanted to water ski. And I distinctly recall you being the one to pull Ryan off from the edge of the gondola when he nearly tumbled into the water, almost sending you in with him." He swung their arms. "What amazed me was your enjoyment of the experience. And don't get me started on the stories you told me on our first date."

She shrugged as if that were no big deal. "Okay, so I like a bit of excitement. My parents instilled it into me. But I also appreciate a sense of togetherness. It's what Conrad offered, and I took it."

Lanelle wondered if Dante was aware he was squeezing her fingers. "Did you love him?"

"I thought with time I'd fall in love with him, but I never did."

He relaxed his grip.

"Even without passion or a true love, we had a good marriage. I could rely on him. And when I got pregnant we were ecstatic."

"Pregnant?"

Lanelle nodded, attempting to push down the lump that had formed in her throat. Years later and it still affected her.

"You have a child?"

And the knife twisted. *I won't cry.* She fought back the sting of tears. She'd gotten through it, and now she'd tell the story without giving in to the torment she'd gone through. "No. The babies died." She let go of his hand and wrapped her arms around her waist, squeezing tight. An onslaught of pain ripped through her at the memory.

"Can I hold you?" She barely heard his low voice. "Please?"

She made the affirmative movement of her head so slight she hoped he wouldn't be able to see it. Wanting someone to comfort her so desperately could only lead to heartbreak, but she refused to deny herself.

Releasing her arms from around herself, she sank into him as he cradled her. The rhythmic thudding of his heart beneath her ear calmed her. His hand rubbing up and down her back gave her a combined sense of warmth, home and security she'd never experienced.

Taking a shuddering breath as tears slid down her cheeks, she finished the dreaded story. "The first one died of a spontaneous abortion at five months. We got pregnant again." She sniffled. "With twins. They were delivered at seven months, but they…" Lanelle swallowed the pain in her throat. "Not even the care of the best NICU staff could help them. Each had survived for a couple of days."

Chapter 16

Every word Lanelle spoke clawed into Dante's soul. Why should one person have to suffer so much?

Holding her made the world fall away. He waited for her tears to abate as his heart broke for the young woman she'd been.

"Even the steadiest person can fail you." She tilted her head up. "With every child I lost, my world crumbled."

The pain in her eyes too much for him to endure, he lowered his lashes as he took a fortifying breath. By the time he opened them, her head rested on his chest.

"Conrad supported me the whole time. I knew I'd married a good man, and his actions proved it. I wanted to love him so much that I made myself believe I did. But it was a lie."

He held her a little tighter.

"Within three months of the twins'—" she swallowed "—deaths, he divorced me. And less than two months later he was remarried."

"Bastard."

She looked into his face, the shadow of a smile tilting the corners of her lips upward. "Exactly. But it's not even the worst of it. The woman ended up having twins. Perfectly healthy."

The sobs shook her body. Her gut-wrenching tears caused Dante's own throat to throb with pain as he cried over the woman who'd lost her children.

Lanelle's legs no longer supported her. As she sagged against Dante, without warning her feet left the ground. Her gaze rose up to witness his tear-filled eyes. Too wrung out to command him to put her down, she snuggled against his chest.

She opened her eyes as he settled her onto his lap once he'd sat on a park bench. How long had he walked holding her?

Placing a finger under her chin, he lifted her head to look at him. "I don't have the power to take away your pain or to bring back your children. If I could I would. I promise you."

She believed him. Needed him. Curling her arms around his neck, she clung, wishing he'd never let her go. For the next few minutes, he didn't. She pulled away first.

Shouldn't she feel self-conscious after having cried her heart out? Especially over something that had happened over five years ago. She should be over it by now, or at least better able to control her emotions.

Lanelle waited for the shame to hit, but it never came. Climbing off his lap, she stood and tested her weight on her feet. Steady.

He got up, ensuring she didn't fall by holding her shoulders.

"Thank you for listening."

His gaze held hers. "Anytime."

With a hand to her stomach, she summoned a grin. "I'm exhausted. Are you ready to go back?" She hoped the question didn't sound as curt as it came out, after he'd spent the night listening to the drama that used to be her life.

"Of course. Let's go to the main street and get a taxi."

She frowned. How many times in her life would she be in this glorious city? "It's a lovely night. I'm not too tired to walk."

He led her in the direction from which she presumed they'd come. At one point he held out his hand to her. Lanelle wanted more from him. She sought the strength his body could provide, so she looped her arm around his waist and laid her head against him.

Draping an arm around her, he whispered, "Did you name the babies?"

Lanelle brought her head up at the question. His free hand cupped her cheek and returned her head to his shoulder. "The first one was a boy. Conrad and I went back and forth on it, but we eventually decided to name him Dominic Conrad Murphy."

"You kept your ex's last name?"

Lanelle shrugged, choosing not to explain she'd done it to avoid the notoriety of her parents' names. She didn't want him to recognize her for the heiress status she possessed, so she kept her family's surname to herself.

Lanelle didn't seek anything more from him than what he'd offered her tonight, but she liked that he didn't know her true identity. If any of what they shared was real, then it would be because he liked *her*, not her parents' empire or her own millions.

Settling on a half-truth, she said, "It pissed him off to no end when I told him I'd keep his last name, so I couldn't resist. Toshia egged me on the whole time."

Dante chuckled. "What about the twins?"

"Girls. We didn't discuss what we'd name them. But when I held them in my arms as they took their dying breaths, I named one Angela and the other Destiny, figuring they'd go to heaven and be the angels they'd been destined to become."

He squeezed her closer as they walked.

"Do you think you'll have children?"

She knew Dante wanted kids, if only to pass on his and Mr. Calvano's legacy. After seeing how he interacted with Vanessa and Ryan, she'd realized that the need to bestow love onto others spurred his decision, too. It would be better for him to find out now rather than later. "I… I can't."

"Because it would be too hard?"

At her attempt to pull away, he didn't stop her. He did brace her shoulders in a gentle grip and turned her to face him.

"It would be impossible," she admitted, leaving out that it might kill her if she lost another child.

A step backward stopped his hands from burning her skin. She resumed walking toward the hotel, eyes dry and head held high. She spoke before he could ask any more questions. "That's life, right? It goes on." *Even when you think it's come to an end and you no longer want it to.*

Over the years, the pain had dulled as her heart hardened. Until Dante's impromptu arrival. He'd somehow melted the glacier bit by bit. What kind of woman would she be if she limited him from procreating? He was too good of a man not to pass his genes on. And what about his company and the Calvano name?

"Why? What did the doctors say happened to the twins?"

Although tempted to not tell him the truth, she figured he deserved to know. "Conrad had the rhesus, or what is commonly called Rh, factor in his blood, while I don't," she stated clinically. "I'm Rh negative. When my first child was born, they discovered he was Rh positive. I was given a vaccine called RhoGAM so I wouldn't produce antibodies against the blood of the next baby if he or she inherited Conrad's positive factor."

His nod prompted her.

"They say it's extremely rare, but the vaccine didn't work. I produced antibodies. The twins were both Rh positive and—" she tapped her chest "—my own body attacked them, making them so severely anemic they were born too weak to survive. Of course, we didn't learn any of this until they were struggling for their lives. Not even Conrad's blood donation helped."

Understanding seemed to dawn when he sucked in air through his mouth.

"Yes, it's the reason Conrad left me. The chances of us having a healthy child together weren't good." In some ways she didn't blame her ex for dumping her. And yet she'd lost respect for him for doing it.

"But you could've had children other ways. Surrogacy. Adoption." He flailed his hands. "I don't know. Something."

She knew all of that. When Conrad had made it clear that he was leaving her because he needed children from his seed, she'd offered to go the surrogacy route. He'd refused, claiming to be too much of a traditionalist, and that any child he had would be carried by its mother, not a stranger. His words had stabbed her in the heart.

Of course, if Dante was Rh negative, she could deliver ten healthy children if they wanted, but a bone-chilling fear kept her from spilling the words. What if he left her brokenhearted one day?

She needed him to let her go so she wouldn't long for him. For the family he might be able to give her. For his love. She wanted the safe and protected life she'd built since Conrad left, with no risk of losing what she held most dear. Angling her head, she hit him with "Aren't you the same person who wants biological children to pass down the Calvano name and legacy to? Conrad wanted the same. From his wife's womb."

"But—"

She stopped him with a finger to his lips. "It's okay. Everything happens for a reason, right?" She'd spent the last few years trying to convince herself of it and didn't need him feeling guilty for wanting what she wouldn't give him. "Let's get back."

They walked the rest of the way in silence. The beauty of the city's nightlife had left her sight. At her room, her hands shook as she fumbled with the key card and slid it into the slot. With the green light and accompanying click, she pushed the door open.

She bit the inside of her cheek as she regarded him. "Thanks for the walk and listening ear."

"Can I give you a kiss good-night?"

Her stomach tumbled at both the question and the humility with which he'd asked it. What would be the point? *None, other than pure pleasure.*

"Please?" Would he always be able to break her down?

In response she stepped toward him. He met her the rest of the way. Without laying a hand on her, he leaned down and touched his lips against hers in what she could only describe as a butterfly kiss. So light and fleeting it barely existed. He removed his mouth and repeated the action twice. "Those are for the three children who will forever be in your heart."

The next kiss gave her enough time to respond to the pressure, but it flittered away too soon. "For the children you should've been blessed to bear without the torment of not knowing if they'll survive," he whispered.

Placing his hands on her hips, he returned to the place she needed him most. This time the kiss seared her as he teased her lips. When she opened to him, she expected him to deepen it.

He released her lips and stood erect, gazing down at her. What had that one been for? She'd never know because he unwound her arms from his neck without telling her.

"Good night, Lanelle. If you need anything, don't hesitate to call. I'll always be available for you."

What she wanted was for him to extend the kisses into something more. Not trusting her ability to speak, she raised her hand and waved. Repressing the urge to rush into his arms, she utilized all her energy and stepped backward into the room.

Once inside she caught her breath, overwhelmed by the strength of his presence. How would she be able to get him out of her system now? For his sake, she had to. She would.

Lanelle may never be able to bear kids. My children. Her reaction during their first date made sense. He'd told her he wanted children. They would carry on Mr. Calvano's legacy. Dante covered his face and forced his head back. What had he done? He'd hurt her. Badly.

The carpet absorbed his weight as he paced. No wonder she'd stayed the hell away from him. In no uncertain terms he'd told her they had no future because of his need for children.

Would she be willing to have a child with a surrogate or adopt? From the way she'd reacted when he'd brought it up, the options didn't seem viable to her. Or had that been a residual reaction from the influence of her selfish ex-husband?

Could he be with Lanelle, knowing his business might no longer end up in his direct line of descent?

He had nephews and nieces he could leave it to if they showed interest. If the worst occurred, he could find a protégé, as Mr. Calvano had. But he didn't want anyone going through the same type of hell in his legal battle with the Calvano family. People, especially family, tended to get greedy when it came to money.

Dante had sent up a prayer of gratitude for Mr. Calvano's decision to choose him as a successor every day since his first trip to Italy.

Would having only Lanelle in his life be enough? Did he need children of his flesh and blood to fulfill him? These were questions he never thought he'd ask because he'd always presumed he'd have a family.

This strong emotion, which he recognized as love, never wavered. Everything about Lanelle made him happy. Even her obstinate nature, although annoying when directed against him, showed that she could stand her ground at all times. She was someone who'd always have his back without succumbing to the needs of others over his.

Of course, she'd probably put her own first. Was she the type of woman to compromise? And most important, was she honest? One thing he could never tolerate was someone who thought him fool enough to lie to him. He wouldn't have it. He had so much to learn about her.

First he had to figure out if he'd be wasting both of their time by getting involved with her. As he pulled back the reins on the team of horses storming off with his thoughts, it hit him that maybe she had no interest in him.

The lingering heat from her sweet lips didn't lie, yet perhaps she sought his comfort only after such an arduous admission.

He couldn't spend all night contemplating Lanelle and her ways. Tomorrow would be soon enough to come up with solutions after a good night's sleep.

Chapter 17

Entering the town of Carrara always infused Dante with a natural high. Unable to sit in the vehicle for a moment longer, he ordered the driver to pull over as they crested a hill. When the van he'd chartered to pick them up from the airport stopped, Dante hopped out. He inhaled as much fresh air into his lungs as he could tolerate. If not for the fact he'd pass out, he had no desire to exhale.

"I didn't think he'd be *this* bad," Vanessa said.

Dante ignored her, continuing to revel in the place bringing peace to his being. He searched the small group. The other balm to his soul stood in the opposite direction. He went to Lanelle and bumped her shoulder with his. "What do you think?"

"It's wonderful. Serene and quaint."

He pointed to one of the quarries in the distance. "We get our marble from there."

At her nod, he wondered why he hadn't kissed the long, elegant curve of her neck last night. She'd returned to being aloof when he'd seen her in the morning, and with the preparations to leave Milan, they hadn't had a chance to talk.

Lanelle turned to meet his gaze. She opened her mouth

to speak, then closed it without saying a word as they stared at each other. He inched toward her, finding her magnetic pull too strong to resist.

Ryan's voice intruded as he tugged Dante's pant leg. "Are you sure I can't climb the rocks?"

Dante straightened with a frustrated growl before leveling his nephew with the strictest look he could muster. "No, you cannot." He enunciated each word. "That's my final word on the subject, so stop asking. Let's get back in the van."

The boy picked up a stone and threw it. "You mean we aren't there yet?"

Placing an arm around Ryan's small shoulders, Dante guided him to the vehicle. "I wanted to show you the town from a vantage point. What do you think of it?"

Ryan shrugged, obviously having no opinion on the matter.

Vanessa joined them. "It's cool, but I don't see why you go on and on over it."

Dante's hand went to his chest as he gasped. "The marble extracted from here is exquisite."

"Yeah, yeah, yeah. Mom and Dad are waiting for us. Is it just me, or have they been all lovey-dovey since we got to Italy?"

Dante looked at Lanelle. "Must be something in the air."

They trooped into the van and rode the short distance to town. At the hotel, his family disembarked from the vehicle and rushed out of the sweltering heat into the building. Dante lingered behind. Prior to Mr. Calvano's death, he'd stayed with him at his villa. A heaviness settled in Dante's chest at the acute sense of loss for the man who'd helped carve him. He ducked his head as he wiped a tear at the memory of his mentor and Italian father.

Lanelle stepped beside him. "Are you okay?"

He sniffled, then cleared his throat. "I'm fine."

Then the unexpected happened. She opened her arms to him. He'd take any opportunity to be near her, so he held her close. Similar to what he'd done for her last night, she rubbed his back. "You miss Mr. Calvano."

Dante inhaled the exotic, floral scent he now identified with Lanelle. Why hide the truth? "Yes."

After a few more seconds of appreciating her soothing fingers, he slid his hands down her back to her hips before summoning the strength to release her. "Thank you."

With a quick nod and a pat on his shoulder, she turned to join the others inside the exclusive hotel, making him fall deeper in love as she went.

After a sumptuous lunch of ravioli stuffed with mushrooms and beef, topped with what had to be the best marinara sauce Lanelle had ever tasted, she skipped the nap everyone else, except for Dante, decided to indulge in. He'd slipped out of the hotel for a business meeting.

She sighed, wishing she'd gone with him. With each minute they spent together, she had more difficulty keeping whatever they had platonic.

Rather than dwell on not being able to keep such a fantastic man in her life, she made a work call to the United States. As much money as she had to her name, she hated spending it on roaming charges. When her personal accountant picked up, she didn't mince words. "What have you found out?"

He'd been shadowing the forensic accountant. "The guy you hired is a genius. He picked up a few discrepancies we didn't. The hospital released the bids only yesterday, so we're going through them."

Lanelle scooted to the edge of the brocade-upholstered

seat. She'd had to get tough with the president of the board and had insisted they release the bids to her accountant immediately. The man wasn't stupid; he knew that if he angered her, the chances for any further funding from the Astacio family would be cut off. "Let's hope we get the evidence we need to find the culprit. I hate thinking that someone could've gotten away with stealing all of that money." *My money.*

Her gut screamed that procurement fraud had occurred right under her nose and she'd been too busy to see it. Not for a moment did she regret helping her father, but she should've paid more attention to the project of her heart.

"So do I," Jay said. "With this guy you've hired, we're sure to get to the bottom of it. Someone will be doing jail time for theft when this is over."

Lanelle calmed at the reassurance. "Thank you for your hard work."

Her primary personal accountant for the past ten years chuckled. "I should thank you for the opportunity to learn about forensic accounting firsthand."

"Good. It means you won't be leaving me to snoop into other people's financial issues."

"Keep treating me like you do and you'll have no worries. How's Italy?"

Lanelle smiled. "It's brilliant, but I'll have to tell you more about it when I get back. This call is costing me a fortune."

Jay snorted but didn't reply. "Have fun. And don't worry, we'll figure out what happened."

"I know we will. Bye."

Lanelle sat as she hung up and rested her head against the back of the chair. She'd get to the bottom of whatever was going on and then make the culprits pay, with interest.

She'd let Jay worry about it for now. Her main concern was keeping Mr. Sanderson out of places he didn't belong. Like her heart.

Chapter 18

With his wild gestations and dramatic voice rising and lowering as if in a play, Dante seemed to take great delight in orating the history of Carrara marble. He played the role of a guide on a tour of the quarry once the blazing sun had gone down enough so it wouldn't singe their hair.

Somehow the words "anarchism among the stone carvers" had made it into Lanelle's head, but the explanation hadn't. She'd ask Dante about it later. *Or I could stay away from him and look it up online.* The second option appealed more.

The tour had been wasted on her, but she was pleased to see how much Vanessa liked learning about the quarry and the processing of marble. The questions the young woman asked seemed to impress her uncle.

"Lanelle?"

A small hand slipped into hers. She looked down at the cutest little boy she'd ever had the pleasure of getting to know. She and Ryan had a slow start in warming up to each other. They were more alike in personality than she and Vanessa, and both seemed to crawl rather than sprint when it came to trusting others.

"Yes, Ry."

"Why are you quiet today? You didn't holler at me when I got caught climbing."

She chuckled. "Did you need another person to yell at you?"

"No."

"How about if I scold you now for doing something you know you shouldn't have been doing?"

A broad grin dimpled his cheek. "Come here." Bending, she lifted him into her arms with a grunt. His legs wrapped around her waist as he laid his head on her shoulder rather than fighting to get down as she'd anticipated. Her little lost angels came to mind. Blinking back tears, she choked out, "Why are you smiling?"

He lifted his head and looked into her eyes. "Because it means you love me when you shastricrise me. That's what Mommy says."

It took Lanelle a second to figure out the word Ryan had butchered. Then she smiled. "It's 'chastise.' And even when we don't yell, we still love you."

"Yeah. Vanessa loves me the most. She's always shouting at me and telling me what to do."

She nodded. "I think you're right."

Dante stepped beside them. "Why are you carrying my nephew like a baby?"

Ryan stiffened. "I'm not a baby."

"Then get down and walk."

Ryan's deep sigh indicated he'd enjoyed being carried. With one last squeeze of her neck, he loosened his legs and slid down, running toward his parents.

"You pamper him," Dante charged.

Emotion overwhelming her, Lanelle avoided looking at him. "We all do. He's a good kid. If a little rambunctious at times." She kicked a stone, sending it skipping away. "He's almost a year older than my oldest would've been."

Without seeking permission this time, he wrapped her

in a hug. Lanelle soaked up his comforting warmth before remembering just how much she shouldn't need his touch. Shoving herself away, she tucked a strand of wind-blown hair behind her ear.

Dante steered them in the direction of the others. "I'll have to discuss it with the rest of our crew, but I wanted your opinion first."

She viewed his profile as she waited for him to speak. His nose had the cutest little flare at the nares.

"One of the people I've worked with for years suggested we spend a few days in Rome and the rest of the vacation in Sicily. What do you think?"

Why was he asking her? She'd go wherever they led her on this adventure. "Why Sicily?"

"The guy is from there, and he talks about it all the time. He says it's a restorative place."

"How so?"

He lifted both shoulders to his ears and held the pose for a couple of seconds before releasing them. Lanelle stifled a giggle. So Ryan got the gesture from him.

"I didn't ask," he said, "but after searching the internet, it seems like a great place. I recall Mr. Calvano encouraging me to visit there, but I was so focused on work when I came that I never bothered." He gazed out into the horizon. "We could do some island hopping, sightsee or just lie on the beach all day."

Lanelle thought about the potential within the change in plans. Perhaps if they weren't running all over Rome, she'd get to spend more time alone with Dante and get to know him a little better. *Or you could stay the hell away from him, like you've been doing.*

"What do you think of the idea?"

She hitched a shoulder, hoping to give off a vibe of indifference, although excitement bubbled up within her, happy he was interested in her opinion. "It's your dime."

His deft fingers skittered along her bare arm until they reached her hand and held it. A delicious shiver ran up her spine. "I'd like to know if you think it's a good idea."

Pulling her thoughts back from the fringes of pleasure, she said, "It's a good idea. Rome is sure to be crowded and busy, which might not be the best for any of us. Well, except for Ryan. From what you mentioned, Sicily sounds like a good place to relax."

As if in slow motion, he brought her hand up to glide his lips across the knuckles. "Thank you."

Lanelle could get used to his gentle and affectionate ways. "You're welcome."

As she and Dante walked hand in hand toward the others, she didn't bother to pull away from him. Overriding her heart wouldn't be possible without some sort of surgery. She'd have to ride the wave to see if she'd glide onto the shore or tumble in head over ass.

Dante almost felt badly about squirreling Lanelle away from his family. He'd been on the cusp of turning to join them when Ryan's pout made its appearance. They'd arrived in Rome two days ago after their overnight trip from Carrara and had been roaming the city as a tight unit.

The air rushed through Lanelle's hair, pulling strands out of her ponytail as she pedaled hard in an attempt to beat him in the race she'd initiated. He'd definitely made the right decision to spend uninterrupted time with her.

He pushed a little harder and reached the designated point before her. "I win."

Chest rising and falling with the exertion she'd set into trying to best him in the bike race, she panted, "Unfair advantage."

He raised his brows. "Are you calling me a cheater?"

She laughed, raised her arms in the air and set her face

to the sun. His heart caught at how glorious she looked. Then she looked at him. "Your legs are longer than mine."

He laughed at her logic as he relished being with her.

With her hands back on the handlebars, she stood on the pedals, lifting herself from the seat as they rolled down the road. "The bike tour was a great idea."

They'd taken the more adventurous route on their tour through Rome. He appeased his guilt for leaving the others to undertake their own tour by saying, "Ryan couldn't have handled this route."

Lanelle nodded. "I could barely handle it. But it was so much fun rushing down the hill."

"Even when you wiped out?" His heart had leaped to his throat when she'd tumbled off the bike onto the dirt path.

She raised her arm where the abrasion she'd sustained from elbow to wrist had stopped bleeding. "We were near the bottom, so it wasn't too bad. I didn't care for the rock killing my buzz, though."

He'd anticipated her having a good time on this outing. Yesterday they'd spent the day with the family shopping and touring the Colosseum. Hanging out with the others made it easy for Lanelle to avoid him, so he'd taken the initiative, making plans to get them alone. Executive decisions were what he did best.

"What's on the agenda for our last day in Rome tomorrow?"

They rode closer to the edge of the road as a car passed. "The family is going to a children's museum to keep Ryan from whining. And we're taking a handmade pasta cooking and dessert making course."

She frowned. "I can't see Ryan sitting still while making pasta. Why are we separating again?"

Because I want you all to myself, you beautiful, frustrating woman. When we're with the family, you cling to Vanessa as if you're her chaperone. He gave a safer answer than the one his mind had wanted to spurt out. "To give them a chance to do things together as a family. Soon Vanessa will no longer be a student commuting from home. She'll be out of the house, and opportunities like this will come few and far between. I'm sure Alan and Cynthia want to relish them while they can."

Lanelle nodded. "So I'm stuck with you?"

For a moment, he stopped pedaling as the bike careened forward. At the slight quirk of her lips and the gleam in her eyes, he knew she didn't mind. Rather than answer, he said, "I'll give you a chance to redeem your loss. Race you to the top of the incline."

She huffed out a breath as she looked ahead. "You're on. Call it."

He loved her competitive spirit. They'd been riding over the Roman countryside for the past three hours, and he was exhausted. Her tenacity spurred him on. Making sure they were parallel, he said, "On your mark. Get set. Go!" It wasn't in his nature to let anyone win on purpose, so he pedaled hard to reach the top, but she beat him by a tire.

"What do I win?" she panted.

Dante didn't even pretend to think. "All I have to offer is a kiss." He'd been dreaming about it for the past three days. Being around her but not with her had been torture.

She swallowed, and he feared she'd decline. Then she stopped the bike and straddled it with both feet flat on the asphalt. "I accept."

Wasting no time, he swung his leg over the back of the bike while still in motion and laid it down as he rushed to her side. Hunger and need drove him to capture her lips in a hard kiss as he framed her face with his hands. She clasped onto his shoulders as she opened for him. The hot, wet kiss turned into something that would better serve them behind closed doors.

Making love to her outside in the capital of the homeland of his heart wouldn't be the wisest decision. Dante slowed down the kiss with teasing nibbles of her lips, appreciating every nuance of their fullness. He gave her one last nip before forcing himself to back away. Her whimper didn't make it easier. "Your prize has been claimed."

She opened her eyes and blinked in rapid succession. Then clarity replaced the glaze. "Wanna race again?"

He chuckled as he picked up his bike. "I'd rather not see you go tumbling down another hill. I like your skin on your body, not the ground."

"Spoilsport," she murmured and took off at a leisurely pace with a smile plastered on her face.

He hoped tomorrow they'd get more of a chance to talk, but the day had been extraordinary, just being in her presence as they took in the majesty of the land. He'd learned the serious side she'd been showing him hid a woman of great hilarity. Lanelle laughed at anything and everything that struck her as funny.

A woman after his own heart, but then he already knew that. Time to make sure she did, too. He'd read up on Rh factor and the effects it had on a child in the womb. She hadn't been dramatic when she said her body had attacked her twins.

All he had to do was get a simple blood test done to know if he could have children with her who would survive. Why hadn't he done it yet?

Because it didn't matter. He wanted her, whether they could produce kids together or not. He'd get tested, but whatever the outcome, he'd have Lanelle in his life. If only she'd have him.

Chapter 19

The next morning, Lanelle found it unbearable to sit as she attempted to get out of bed when a knock sounded on the door. Forgoing her conventional way of rising, she rolled onto her stomach and slid her legs off until her feet hit the floor. The move cost her no small amount of pain, making her limp to the door at another knock and Vanessa's voice floating through the door. "Lanelle, it's me."

She opened the door to find Dante standing behind his niece. He rushed past Vanessa to Lanelle's side, his brows creased with concern. "What's wrong?"

She chuckled when she wanted to groan in pain. "I overdid it on the bike." She shrugged. "Consequences." He guided her to the armchair, but she bristled at sitting on it. Her behind had never felt so sore. Then she noticed Dante's smooth motions. "Why aren't you in pain?"

"Uncle D is a cyclist," Vanessa answered. "He's even won a few medals."

Lanelle glared at him. "You could've told me this before you issued those challenges."

He performed his adorable Ryan shrug, and she forgave him the duplicity. His voice went low and husky. "I could let you claim more prizes if you'd like."

Remembering the kiss sent a shiver of anticipation down her spine. If only Vanessa weren't staring at them, she'd take him up on the offer. If she weren't so sore, she'd make sure it went further than those searing kisses.

She snapped herself out of her thoughts, wondering where they'd come from. Nothing had changed. They weren't dating. Nor would they because she couldn't give him what he needed. Too heart- and butt-sore to continue standing, she went to the bed and flung herself onto it. Lanelle moaned with relief as her muscles unclenched. "I won't be going anywhere today."

Vanessa sat on the side of the bed. "I'll stay with you."

"No, you won't," Lanelle insisted. "How many opportunities will you get to visit Rome? I'll be all right. A couple of ibuprofen and a warm pack in an unmentionable place and I'll be fine."

Vanessa laughed. "Are you sure?"

"One hundred percent. Now go take Rome by storm and take loads of pictures."

The young woman stood. "Feel better."

Dante stayed by her bedside. "If I had known we'd be riding for so long…"

Lanelle grinned. "I loved every minute of it and would do it again. Maybe with bike shorts on next time." She pointed a finger straight up. "Extra padding and maybe a chair seat, too."

Dante didn't look convinced. Without a word, he followed Vanessa out.

Ten minutes later, Lanelle was still contemplating the best way to reach over to the other side of the bed so she could call the front desk to have them send her medication and food when the door swung open. Her martial arts training had her standing before the pain registered.

Arms filled with a food-laden tray, Dante walked in and set it on the table. "Are you always so jumpy?"

"Only when people enter my room without knocking."

"Sorry, I left the door open a little before I went down so I could get right back in."

He kept his gaze glued to her as she settled back in bed. "I should've known something was wrong when you didn't come down for breakfast. You never miss a meal." The crinkles in the corners of his eyes showed up. "Or a snack."

The giggle burst from her at his correct assessment.

He went to her side. "I brought you breakfast, ibuprofen and a hot-water bottle."

Her heart melted at the sweetness of his gesture. Then he held out his arm. "Hold onto me and I'll prop you up so you're lying at an angle and you can eat." She did as he instructed. Taking the pill from him, she downed it with a sip of orange juice.

He handed her the covered hot-water bottle. Lanelle had no shame when it came to placing it on her backside, leaning over to the side a little so she wouldn't squish it completely and end up with a wet bed.

She eyed how he'd set everything up by pulling the table to the side of the bed. Yet not where she could reach it. "You aren't feeding me."

Just as he was going to argue, he placed the tray on his lap so she could reach the food. After a few bites of strawberry crepes she'd punch through a cement block for, she asked, "How did you know what I'd like?"

He arched a brow. "Is there anything you don't like when it comes to food?"

She chewed on a piece of sausage and washed it down with a sip of tea, her preference over coffee; she hadn't realized he'd noticed that about her. But then again, nothing should shock her about this extraordinary man.

Lanelle cleared the plate, leaving the obligatory scraps, and then she did away with those, too. She regretted not being able to spend the day with him. "So what are you doing today?"

He considered her as he pulled the table back to its original position with the tray on top. "I've never been officially trained, but I figured I'd nurse a woman who overdid it with a bike ride back to health."

She snorted. "I'm sure there are better things to do with your day."

"Than wait on you hand and foot? Doubtful."

"I'm a very bad patient."

He sat in the chair he'd drawn close to the bed. "Maybe you've never had the right nurse."

She shut her mouth. Why try to get rid of him when all she wanted was for him to stay? So she relaxed into the bed, hoping her smile wasn't as broad as it felt.

Dante had been in stitches all morning as Lanelle unleashed her sense of humor with stories about her brothers and experiences growing up in a boarding school. Of course, she had to wipe away a few tears when he told her some of the more amusing experiences in his repertoire.

She sat without wincing. "I feel much better. A warm bath might be in order."

Only one part of his body stirred at the thought of Lanelle naked and luxuriating in the bathtub. And then the blood returned to the head containing his cerebrum and he stood. "I'll prepare one for you."

"I'm not an invalid."

"Of this I am well aware, but you are my special patient for the day. Your wish is my command."

A sly grin lit her face. "Be careful what you offer, Mr. Sanderson. You never know what I'll ask of you."

My heart, my life, my future. It's all yours. "Point taken. How about your wish within reason?"

Lanelle stood. "Now, that sounds more like the flooring tycoon I've come to know."

He couldn't recall running a bath for a woman before. From the movies and television shows he'd watched on occasion, he knew bath salts and bubbles were in order. He read the directions on the bottles the hotel provided and poured them into the running water. The scents of lavender and vanilla hit his nostrils.

As difficult as he'd found it to not tuck her into his side while she lay in bed, she'd be irresistible after this soak. When the water had filled the tub to a suitable level, he left the bathroom and announced, "Your bath is ready. I even turned the jets on." He gazed at her, wanting her more by the moment. "Need any help?" He winked to let her know he was joking, and yet a serious tinge edged his voice. "Undressing perhaps?"

He didn't miss the way she licked her lips as if the idea held a great deal of appeal. At least that's how he chose to interpret it. "I…" She cleared her throat. "I can handle it on my own." She picked up the clothing she must have collected while he was running the water and getting lost in the imagery of her slick body in the tub.

Her hobbled walk wasn't even half as sexy as normal and yet he couldn't stop watching until she disappeared behind the door. *A grip, boy. Get one.* "I've got some work to do in my room. I'll be back in about thirty minutes."

"Okay."

Damn, how he wished she had invited him to join her.

With her muscles relaxed after a glorious soak in the tub, Lanelle hesitated to return into her room. The hunger she'd witnessed in Dante's eyes as he'd half joked about undressing her made her consider the offer. All she'd wanted was his hands roaming over her body.

She squared her shoulders and opened the bathroom door to find the room empty. At least now she no longer walked as if she'd spent hours astride a horse. She giggled as she sat on the chair Dante had spent the morning in. Toshia would laugh her own behind off about this.

A knock on the door had her standing again. This time, all pain was forgotten as she anticipated seeing Dante. He'd left her side only a short time ago, and she already missed him. Maybe if he weren't so caring and entertaining, she wouldn't be falling—

She halted the thought. When she opened the door and her breath hitched at the sight of him, she knew she wouldn't be able to sit in her room with him without engaging in a sneak attack of his delicious kisses, and maybe more. "What time is the cooking class?"

He blinked at her abrupt question and then looked down at his watch. "It starts at one." He eyed her with suspicion. "Are you feeling up to going?"

Lanelle couldn't stay holed up with him a minute longer. A quick glance at the wall clock told her it was twelve. "Is the place far? Do you think we can make it in time?" Then she remembered how efficient he could be. "Did you cancel the reservation?"

"No. Yes. And no."

"Good. Let me get my purse, and we can be on our way."

"As your nurse, I don't think this is a good idea."

As a hormone-driven woman who needs to be in a public place while with you, it's a brilliant one. "I'm fine now. The rest, painkillers and bath did me a world of good." So what if he didn't believe her? They were going. "Plus, learning how to make fresh pasta is something I never knew I wanted to learn how to do until you mentioned it."

"Fine." Then he pointed a warning finger in her direction. "Don't say I didn't warn you."

Lanelle rolled her eyes Vanessa-style, then pushed him out the door to experience another aspect of Italy with the man who'd dug himself deeper under her skin.

Chapter 20

"This place is paradise. Look how clear the water is." Lanelle walked into the warm yet refreshing ocean as they left the family she'd come to love lounging on the pristine beach. Lifting her hand, she allowed water to slip through her fingers. She'd been to Trinidad once with her parents and remembered the water as a brilliant blue. The Mediterranean surpassed the Atlantic's beauty in both color and transparency. The spectacular aqua blue amazed her. "I think the whole family is enjoying Sicily. Great change in plans, Dante." They'd come to the beach as soon as they'd landed that afternoon.

"Thanks."

As she walked into the water up to her thighs, she could feel his eyes on her. In her younger years she would've worn a bikini, but her growing love of fine cuisine encouraged a one-piece, even though she knew she'd still look good in a two-piece. "I could've done with a bit more pasta making in Rome. It was so delicious." Their date yesterday had been fun and educational. Watching Dante cook had ratcheted him up on the sexiness meter, though she could've sworn he'd already reached the maximum level.

"So I noticed, when you ate two plates of your home-made linguine for dinner. You could always come back with me to create other kinds. Or attend the Vatican tour you keep moaning about missing."

Her gaze flickered to him. Was he joking? Her nipples puckered at the sight of his bare, muscular chest, dark and smooth; she longed to touch him. Run her tongue over every inch of his body. With haste, she moved farther into the water and dived in. The short swim should take care of the heat being near him had stoked.

What the heck is wrong with me? She couldn't be with him. He hadn't attempted to kiss her again, even though they'd spent the last day in Rome together. His restraint said it all. He'd made his decision to not accept a woman who couldn't bear him children, and she'd respect it. At least her mind would. Her heart and body were having trouble keeping up.

When she couldn't hold her breath any longer, she tentatively brought her feet down, anticipating she'd have to tread water. Her feet hit sand, so she stood. The water reached midchest.

Her confusion must've shown because Dante said, "We're far out but still on the continental shelf. Wait, sorry. Sicily is an island. It's called an insular shelf. It doesn't get deep until we're farther out." He waved his hand to indicate they'd have to swim a long distance.

"Oh." *Isn't he an earth science genius?* Of course he would be. He made his money through nature. A scan of the area revealed that none of the few beachgoers had ventured out this far. She looked out into the endless horizon. Did the sea have an end? Everything had one, didn't it?

She squirmed under his intense stare. "Do you think you'll ever marry again?"

Lanelle's mouth opened and closed twice in a row. Before she could tell him it was none of his business, she released her own question. "Do you plan to hate women who come from rich families for the rest of your life?"

He hissed in a breath as his jaw clenched. "What gave you that idea?"

She narrowed her eyes at him as she glided her hand through the water. "The comment you made about Eliana Astacio."

He crossed his arms over his still-appealing chest. "The shoddy workmanship she allowed in the NICU made me angry."

"No. There was something personal to it." She stepped toward him and touched his biceps. She was hurt when he shook her off and sliced through the water. Tenacity had always been her style, so she followed him.

When he surfaced, she once again eased her feet down to feel for the sandy bottom. The water reached her armpits. "I'm sorry I pried. You asked me a personal question, so I thought I'd give it back to you." *Does it matter that I've been curious about why you hate people of my social standing ever since our second date?*

"Back in college, I got engaged to a woman from old money. It turns out she was slumming it with me when we were on campus and dating someone from her circle while apart during the breaks."

"She was an idiot."

His brows wrinkled together. "Was she? I had nothing at the time. What could I have offered her?"

"Your compassion, sense of humor, intelligence, drive and your love should've been the only things that mattered." *At least it would for me.*

"It didn't. All I know, not just from the experience with my ex, but from business dealings with some of them, too, is that they look down on those of us who have made our riches off the sweat of our brows."

"All of them?"

She held her breath as he considered the question. He'd worked with her father and he would never treat anyone as second-class.

"No, not all, but a lot."

She smiled at his honesty. "Glad to hear."

A splash of water hit her in the face, and she reciprocated with her own. A brief splashing war dispelled the tension until he asked, "What about you?"

She shrugged. "I've never really thought about remarrying."

"Because of the risk of having children again?"

Instead of anger, misery settled into her chest. They could've had children if Conrad had been willing to compromise. "That, and because men aren't reliable."

"Don't you mean your ex wasn't reliable?"

Lanelle stared at him, wondering how he'd take the truth about her identity. "No. Men. When they find out something isn't what they thought it would be or there are glitches that ensure the situation doesn't go the way they want, they take off."

Expecting a battle-of-the-sexes discussion, she relaxed her shoulders when he asked, "Have you dated anyone since you divorced?"

"A few guys casually. Nothing serious."

"Good."

Her heart beat triple time at the tender expression on his face. She walked farther into the water to see if the depth would increase. Only by an inch or so. A few short weeks ago, she would've kept walking in order to get away from the temptation he'd become. His hand on her shoulder didn't frighten her. This revelation alone scared the crap out of her, but she didn't shrug away from his touch. Neither did she sweep his leg, slamming him into the water.

She grabbed his hand and interlaced his with hers. Not trusting their luck that the water wouldn't suddenly become deep and suck them under, she turned to head back toward the shore.

The warmth of Dante's touch sent ripples of need through her, settling at her center. What would it be like to make love to him? She'd never know. Funny how this didn't stop her from wanting to be around him all the time. She should let go of his hand, but only the sudden presence of a shark in the water could make it happen.

He stopped her and reached out with his free hand. Before he made contact with her cheek, he looked into her eyes. "May I?"

She nodded.

Her stomach flipped as he released her hair from its band and ran his fingers through it. "It's so soft."

Her hand landed in his afro, then slid to the shell of his perfect ear. His eyes became hooded.

They lunged toward each other with lips meeting in a wet, openmouthed crush. Hungry desire replaced all thought as their tongues caressed. The kiss became endless, the yearning elevated.

Bodies flush, his arousal pressed into her belly. Her hands roamed down the planes of his chest. Just as hard as she remembered. He groaned when her fingers rubbed against his peaked nipples.

Grabbing his shoulders, she found the buoyancy of the water made it easy to leap up and wrap her legs around him. All thoughts became superfluous but one. *Get closer.*

He wrenched his mouth free. She needed more. The salt water assailed her taste buds as she slid her tongue down his neck and sucked. With a slight loosening of her legs, she modified her position so his erection hit the apex of her thighs. She flung her head back at the pleasure.

His hands held her hips in place as she ground against him. Sliding a hand between them, he shifted her bathing suit and rubbed a thumb over her throbbing clit, making her feel so good. Her breaths came out in short spurts. How many years had it been since she'd been touched like this? Never. The intensity was unprecedented.

It wouldn't take much to have him inside her where she needed him. Of its own volition, her hand reached into his shorts.

At the sound of his moan, reality slapped her in the face. *What am I doing?*

As if he'd realized the same thing, he removed his hands from her as she released her legs from around him, her feet landing in the silky sand. The lack of contact left her bereft.

Panting, they stepped away from each other. The draw between them remained, yet dampened.

He dunked his head under the water. *Good idea.* She did the same, and when she returned to the surface he'd swum a few feet ahead. They'd been so close to having sex on a public beach. Granted, no one could see them from this distance without binoculars, but still.

She flung her hair behind her as she emerged, wiping water off her face. No condom. She would've done it without one and regretted it for months to come. What if she'd gotten pregnant? No, she couldn't bear the heartbreak of another lost baby. Allowing that to happen would be foolhardy. And her parents would never claim a fool as their child.

She dived in again, this time propelling herself away from the lure of Dante toward the shore.

Dante struggled to catch up with Lanelle as her powerful strokes kept her ahead. Hopefully, by the time he reached the beach, his desire and hard-on would be squelched.

What should I say when we meet up? Nothing came to mind. Apologizing was out of the question because he held no remorse. If they'd had a condom handy, she would've been deep in the throes of her orgasm by now. Never had the need to be sheathed inside a woman overtaken him so hard he'd come within a touch of overriding his one and only rule when he had sex.

A casual affair would assuage the passion flaring between them. Not a viable option. At least not for him. He needed her in his life.

Pausing midstroke, Dante flipped onto his back, relaxing his body as the sea encased him. If only making decisions could be as easy as floating. The question of what to do about Lanelle pounded into his head as the small waves lapped over him. Did he want to forgo having children by natural means?

He had to get tested. *Today.* If he ended up having Rh-negative blood, then he could provide her with all the children she wanted. But being positive would mean that if they tried to get pregnant there'd be a great risk of Lanelle's body attacking the baby...their baby.

Dante opened his eyes to find the brilliant sky sprinkled with a few white fluffy clouds. Releasing himself from the water, he stood with caution as he got his bearings. Scanning the shore, he observed his family where they'd left them. Not surprised that Lanelle wasn't among them, he headed their way to tell them he'd take a quick trip to town.

He'd figure out a solution. His future depended on it.

Chapter 21

Lanelle found it difficult to look at Dante. Not due to any sort of discomfiture, but the deep pools of his eyes had a way of luring her in. Okay, so his smoking-hot body and confident gorgeousness contributed, too. And to think those soft, full lips had been on hers. Her shoulders gave an involuntary shimmy at the seductive memory.

Dante had attempted to talk to her after their water incident, but she'd kept it brisk, and she hadn't seen him for the rest of the afternoon. Her cheeks puffed out as she exhaled. How could she have let things get so far? Losing herself to him as if he'd become her sole purpose for existing. Never had she experienced such a barrage of sensations.

Just thinking about the water lapping against them as they—*whew*. Reaching up, she wiped a trickle of sweat off her face.

What she wouldn't give to do it again. This time with a condom showing up out of thin air so they could complete the act.

Snap out of it. Making love to him would be akin to handing over her emotional well-being. She refused to take the risk. He'd break her heart when he inevitably left her to find someone willing to have his children.

After Conrad had walked out, she'd gone to see her doctor about a tubal ligation. Clipping her fallopian tubes would guarantee that she'd never get pregnant and go through the same torturous pain she'd experienced with the loss of her babies. After her doctor's extensive counseling, she'd opted out. She'd been unable to ignore the irreversibility of the procedure when she'd hesitated at the doctor's question: "What if this feeling of doom passes, as it often does, and you want to try for children?"

Thinking about having a child who had Dante's dark skin and sharp features made Lanelle smile as she added a short afro to it. For once the thought of getting pregnant didn't cause her lungs to squeeze tight, leaving her gasping for breath.

As she and Vanessa relaxed, swinging in the cooling night air in the hotel's peaceful garden, the hammock tipped precariously to the side when Vanessa sat up, pointing. "Look, a shooting star. Make a wish." The girl closed her eyes.

Only one request came to Lanelle's mind, and it involved a six-foot-two man with a contagious laugh. Lanelle kept her eyes open as she made her wish.

Vanessa relaxed into the hammock. "What's it like to be in love?"

Lanelle angled her head to get a better look at Vanessa's upturned face as she stared at the constellation-filled sky.

What could she say?

Lanelle closed her eyes, only to see Dante's piercing brown eyes shimmering with tears as he empathized with her past. "With the wrong one, it's as if you lose your very essence in an attempt to be who they want you to be. True love is the opposite. You learn more about who you are and your purpose in life. As if doors have been opened with a key you never knew you had until you met the individual."

"Mmm. Nice. Are you in love with Uncle D?"

She had nothing to gain by denying what she'd shout to the world if she weren't the wrong woman for him. "Yes."

Vanessa turned her head and smiled. "I wondered if you were going to tell me the truth."

"Why did you ask if you knew the answer?"

"To see if you knew it."

A wise young woman. "Have you ever been in love?"

"Not really. Guys I liked a lot, but it never seemed enough to call it love. You know what I mean?"

"I do."

Unlike the cities they'd visited in Italy, Sicily's quiet flowed around them. They'd landed in Agrigento, where they'd toured historic Greek temples. The ancient ruins had Lanelle's imagination in overdrive about what life must've been like during those times.

Unlike her boisterous nature, Vanessa's voice came out soft. "I hope you two will be happy together. I knew you'd be perfect for him when I first met you."

"Really?"

She nodded. "Yup."

"How?"

Vanessa's hand reached upward and clenched as if attempting to collect one of the sparkly pieces sitting millions of years in the past. "I don't know. I just did." Without warning of the change in topic, she said, "I've come close, but never actually, you know…done *it*. What's it like?"

This time it was Lanelle's turn to nearly knock them out of the netting when she sprang up, hoping they were talking about anything other than sex. "Please clarify the *it* for me."

"Sex. I've never had sex. Happy?" Vanessa admitted.

"Why?"

"Definitely not because of Mom and her long-winded abstinence speeches, that's for sure." She let a beat of time pass. "I always imagined it would be special. Even though my friends were having sex, it never seemed right for me. So I didn't."

Resisting the pressure of her peers sounded like something Vanessa would excel at, and Lanelle felt even prouder of her. "I don't care what they write in novels or show in movies." Lanelle crinkled her nose. "The first time, at least for me, was horrible. It hurt, was awkward, and since my partner wasn't considerate, I was left with this lingering need."

"Some of my girlfriends would beg to differ. They said it was wonderful."

"They lied. After the first time, it gets better. Kind of." She'd never been fulfilled by her ex-husband. Before him, the couple of men she'd made love to had been pleasant in bed, but she'd never classify having sex with them as being so good she *had* to have it.

Conrad had taken it to a whole other level by making it just an activity to get through. Practical and predictable to a fault, his main goal in having sex was for him to reach orgasm and ejaculate. Her sexual needs weren't a priority to him and left her unfulfilled. Lanelle recalled making love with him had gotten interesting for a moment a few times, but then like a flash it disappeared.

Toshia would go on and on about the wonders of sex. Lanelle never believed her. Not until the escapade with Dante in the ocean. They'd ravished each other's mouths and practically clawed their skin off to get closer. Giving and taking in equal measures as they drove each other to the brink of extreme need.

Making love to him would truly define the term.

Vanessa chuckled. "What do you mean by 'kind of'? It either does or it doesn't."

"It all depends. If your man is in tune with you, then I've heard it can be great. If not, then…" She let the words trail off.

"How many men have you been with?"

Lanelle put up a front of indignation by waggling her pointer finger. "CocoVan, I have every right not to answer."

"But you will."

"Of course." She'd do almost anything for the young woman who should've been born her baby sister. "Four. Three boyfriends in college, and my ex-husband."

Vanessa shook the hammock as she flipped onto her side, propping her head on her hand. "You were married?"

"A long time ago."

"Whoa. What happened?"

Lanelle expanded her chest with air before plunging into the story. The second time telling it in a few days left her free of tears. Perhaps she was finally learning how to let go of the past.

Meaning she could move into the future. With Dante? No. She wouldn't allow herself to gain a measure of hope in that direction. He expected children from the woman he ended up with.

"Damn." Vanessa fell onto her back. "That's rough. Three deaths? Four, including your marriage. How did you survive?"

She'd asked herself the same question. "We're all meant to go through something."

Vanessa rested her head on Lanelle's shoulder. "Life sucks."

"Sometimes. You ought to know after all you've been through. Being diagnosed with cancer and then kicking its ass." Lanelle raised her hand for a high five, which

Vanessa met. "Other times you wonder at God's magnificence."

"Yeah." The silence extended. "Sorry about losing your babies."

Lanelle released the tears. "Sorry about you having to go through cancer."

Dante covered his yawn just as Lanelle's ended. He never could figure out why the action was so contagious. It didn't help he'd stayed up until three contemplating the results of his blood test.

Today they'd separate. He and Lanelle would stay together while the helicopter he'd hired for the day took the family hopping along the Aeolian Islands, including Vulcano, a popular volcanic island. The sulfur lake it boasted would give Ryan the chance to play in something other than the sea and appease Cynthia's interest in its reputed therapeutic effects. Dante garnered a guess that his sister would dunk Vanessa into the mud like a full-body baptism to ensure she stayed in remission.

Dante nudged his brother-in-law. "Can you please pass the jam?" As he spread some on his toast, he asked, "Are you all excited to swim in the mud baths?"

Ryan spewed out some of the bread in his mouth as he spoke. "Are we really going to swim in mud?"

Vanessa shot a rancid glare at her mother. "Not mud, stinky sulfur."

Cynthia ignored the sparks emanating from her daughter's eyes. "We won't know if it smells until we get there. What will you and Lanelle be doing while we're touring volcanoes and sloshing around in mud?"

He darted a glance toward Lanelle. Meeting her gaze sent his pulse into high gear. He put down the toast he held without taking another bite. "If it's all right with you, I thought we'd head to Trapani." One of the places his Sicilian colleague had sworn to be the most romantic spot on the island. "I've noticed you like churches. The Cathedral of Santissimo Salvatore is there, and I've been told it's worth seeing. Are you up for it?"

Her dark eyes softened, and yet for the longest moment he thought she'd say no. She'd avoided him yesterday. He presumed because she was embarrassed about their make-out session in the sea. Had he scared her away? Maybe it was for the best. *Then why are you whisking her off to Trapani?* A journey to Syracuse would be more exciting, if not a longer car ride.

Dante maintained hope and sought to romance her with old, beautiful churches and breathtaking views of the town and ocean. This was his chance to woo her without his family being around to witness, judge and contribute with annoying suggestions.

"I'm up for it," she finally answered.

"Good. I've been told it's a scenic drive. I think you'll enjoy it."

He didn't miss Vanessa's head moving back and forth between them or when a grin replaced her scowl over having to get dirty in the volcanic sludge.

Trying not to let the anticipation reflect in his voice, he drank the rest of his coffee before saying, "Let's finish up so we can get started. It's going to be an interesting day."

Chapter 22

With no qualms about acting as if nothing had happened between them, Lanelle treated Dante as if it were a normal day on the best vacation she'd ever taken. He hadn't brought *it* up, so she wouldn't, either. She attempted to push down the memory of them together, but it kept surfacing and heating her skin like the blazing sun in the azure sky.

The beautiful landscape as they drove north through the island held her focus. They kept the conversations light. Stories of exploits from his youth and how much trouble he'd gotten into while exploring this country made her laugh so hard her ribs ached.

Lanelle wiped away tears of mirth. "Mr. Calvano had his hands full with you."

"He never told my dad how mischievously I'd behaved. I wasn't troublesome, just curious."

"Makes sense."

"And you? What were you like as a child?"

She hitched the shoulder not restricted by the seat belt. "For the most part quiet. I had my moments of rebellion, though. When I wanted information I'd find it in a logical way, by asking rather than experiencing."

"It doesn't sound like fun."

"It appeased my curiosity and kept me out of trouble." She poked him in the shoulder. "Unlike you."

"It's a good thing I've calmed down in my old age."

She scoffed. "Yeah, what are you, all of twenty-nine?"

"It's good to know I'm still looking young, but I'm a whopping thirty-two."

"Time to settle down, isn't it?" She chewed the inside of her cheek, berating herself for introducing a heftiness to the car's atmosphere. Did she even want to know the answer? She knew it wouldn't be with her, so why be nervous?

He slanted his eyes at her for the briefest of moments and asked, "What about you?"

"Don't you know you're never supposed to ask a woman her age?"

A low rumble of a chuckle came from his throat. "I'm guessing you were one of those nerdy smart-asses in school. I meant about settling down."

"I'm in no rush." She hung her head. Men didn't seem to hang around when their presence was most needed, so why bother?

Thumping his hand on the steering wheel, he spared her a glance. "I keep thinking about the little move you did on me at the fund-raiser."

Lanelle clapped her fingers over her eyes. Would the humiliation of that impulsive moment ever leave her? For almost kissing her, she'd been an infinitesimal twist away from breaking his pinkie. "I'm so sorry," she mumbled.

He reached for her wrist and drew a hand from her face. "Hey, you've already apologized." He slid his hand into hers. "I'm not bringing it up to taunt you. In retrospect it was really cool. Especially since no one else noticed your ability to bring me to my knees. I presume you're some kind of deadly weapon. Are you a black belt supermaster?"

"I don't train for belts, but for knowledge, skills, discipline and health. Ever since high school I've done aikido and Krav Maga."

He whistled. "Damn. That's a wicked combination. I got off lucky."

"I'll say." The roughness of his thumb grazing the back of her hand made her scalp, of all places, tingle.

"I see we've gone past the stage of takedowns as a punishment for touching you," he said, the timbre of his voice deepening.

"Yeah." *Pull over and kiss me.* She focused her attention on the passing homes to avoid uttering the thought. "Other than see the cathedral, what's there to do in Trapani?"

"I know you won't get as excited over this as Ryan, but there's a cable car ride to Erice, which has stunning seaside views."

"You must not know me well, because I'm more excited than Ryan would be. I love heights and seeing beautiful things from above."

Dante chuckled. "Please don't brag about it to him. I'll never hear the end of it."

Lanelle waved a dismissive hand. "I'm the one who should be jealous. They get to travel in a helicopter today. I'm sure his height adventure will supersede mine. What else is there to see?"

"I was told a street called Corso Vittorio Emanuele was the place to be."

"Why?"

"Shopping." He looked at her and winked. "And they have lots of bakeries to choose from."

"So we'll eat. Just like we've been doing the entire trip." Lanelle rubbed her stomach. Not that she'd mention it, but she must have gained at least five pounds so far. Good thing she never got into the craze of wearing skinny jeans. She would've busted out of them.

"And will continue to do until we leave. We're almost there. Where should we go first?"

"The cathedral. I'd like to see what's special about this one." *Other than walking through it with you.* As a pragmatist, romantic notions weren't her thing. Could she ever let go enough to trust someone? To love someone? *Like I already love Dante.*

With his sweet, caring, honest ways, he'd made her fall in love with him.

It didn't matter because nothing would come of it. She refused to bind his life to hers in any way other than her connection with his family.

Kissing was out of the question. With one last longing glance at his tempting lips, she sighed, settled back in her seat and set off to harden herself to their attraction.

She figured the Romans had an easier time building their great city than she would accomplishing this feat.

From his peripheral vision, Dante noticed Lanelle angle herself toward him within the confines of the seat belt. "It seems you know more about me than I do about you."

He took his gaze off the road for a moment for a glance in her direction. "What would you like to know?"

"Tell me something personal about yourself. Just to even the score."

He arched an eyebrow. "Is this a game we're playing?"

"Of course not." Then she shifted her body back to the front. "Forget I asked."

"I didn't think you were the type of person who gave up so easily," he goaded.

Crossing her arms, she ignored him.

"There's nothing much about me you don't already

know. Pretty much what you see is what you get. I live for my family and my work."

"Why aren't you in a relationship?" Lanelle asked after a long pause.

A reciprocal question came to mind. He bit it down. "As far as I can figure, there are two reasons. I'm happily committed to my work. Everyone in my family is always castigating me about it. I'm not just talking about installing flooring, either. I love every aspect of it, including the paperwork. Cynthia claims I've got a type A personality, but I beg to differ. I enjoy being good at what I do. And I do more of it because I like it."

When the silence stretched, Dante thought the question-and-answer session had ended. Then Lanelle asked, "What's the second reason?"

In lieu of being able to look her in the eyes, he placed his hand on her knee. "Up until recently I hadn't found anyone I wanted to commit to. And by that I mean spend every day for the rest of my life with."

"So since your ex-fiancée, you've never had a serious relationship?"

Was she being intentionally obtuse about how he'd just exposed his deepest desire to her? "It's not what I said. I've never felt the need for a happily-ever-after."

Lanelle snorted. "It doesn't exist."

"Doesn't it?"

"No." Lanelle shifted her knee away from him. He took the hint and placed his hand on the steering wheel. "One person ends up leaving. Look at the divorce rates."

He tightened his grip on the steering wheel, wishing it was her ex's neck. "Not all men are like your ex-husband, Lanelle. Not everyone will abandon you, especially when you need them the most." *If you give me a chance, I'll love you until the end of time, and beyond if possible.* He couldn't take the risk of telling her and having her retreat.

Not when they'd gotten a little closer. Time would reveal the truth.

"And remember, not all women who come from money are like the woman who broke your heart."

Where did that come from? Then he recalled the investment work she did. Was she one of the privileged that he'd been bashing? A niggling fear that she hadn't been forthright about who she was made him refuse to ask. Reaching the outskirts of the town, Dante shut down his thoughts, pulled the vehicle over and punched the cathedral's address into the GPS before following the directions to their destination.

Every ancient church they'd toured seemed to calm her. Not overly expressive of her emotions, Lanelle would relax her face, shoulders and overall demeanor when in one. Perhaps it's where she'd derived her strength when life had turned into hell. Better to have her tranquil and present with him than in the aloof mood she'd fallen into after their conversation about exes.

"We're here." The two words were unnecessary, considering they sat in front of a monstrous building that looked like a couple of the others they'd seen.

Lanelle opened the door and slipped out of the car. Her gaze fixed on the cathedral as if she were an angel returning home. She gravitated to the church.

He caught up to her right before she opened the door. As they stepped in, he saw nothing unique about the structure. Stained glass windows, depressed-looking statues and wooden pews. Nothing different from any of the others they'd visited. But the brown and cream marble of the floor caught his interest.

Lanelle's eyes were wide and mouth slightly agape; Dante would've thought she'd seen her favorite movie star. Since there were only a few people sitting in the pews, supposedly praying, he leaned over and whispered into her ear, "Why do you like churches so much?"

When she didn't answer, he touched the small of her back, pleased when she didn't jump away. "Did you hear me?"

Without moving her head, the iris of her eye met the corner. He recognized the look. Her exasperation shouldn't amuse him so much. He let his lips touch the shell of her ear as he asked, "Will you answer?"

He didn't care if she did or not. Being close to her, he could smell the combination of her rose perfume and the faint hint of chocolate. Maybe from the cocoa she drank at breakfast.

"I'll explain later."

Dante backed away. There was no playing when she switched into her no-nonsense mood. Taking a few moments, he looped around the cathedral. Then he sat on one of the benches and proceeded to watch Lanelle observe every aspect of the church.

He watched as she wandered through the building for a good half an hour. What he considered to be a waste of time had her enthralled, which in turn captivated him.

Her beatific smile as she turned to him stole his breath. He'd exist in a state of oxygen deprivation if she looked at him like that every time she saw him.

She swept past without a word. Why did he always have to chase after her? He squinted at the bright sunshine on the other side of the solid engraved wooden doors before sliding on his sunglasses.

Not wanting to risk having the nastier Lanelle come out to play, he didn't ask about the church experience. "I need to get directions on how to reach the cable cars. Unless you aren't interested in going." When had he become hesitant when dealing with a woman? *Since you found one who scares you half to death because you desire her so much.*

Act too macho and she got defensive. But it went against his nature to be some kind of doormat. He pulled his shoulders back and coached himself to man up.

"I'd like to go." She placed a hand over her stomach. "I think eating around the clock has warped my metabolism. I'm hungry again."

"Me, too. Must be the fresh sea air. Let's get to the gas station and ask for directions and a restaurant recommendation." The definitive decision reflected his normal confident, get-it-done personality. Much better than the wuss he'd been a minute ago.

They walked the short distance to the station, where Dante got the instructions for the cable car they'd take to Erice. The clerk didn't seem as impressed by his fluency in Italian as they did on the mainland. In fact, the white-haired old man asked him to repeat himself three times before stating in English, "I can't understand what you're saying. You live on the mainland."

Dante shook his head. "I'm from the States, but I grew up and learned Italian on the mainland."

"It's why I didn't understand you. The dialect is different. See." The man spoke a sentence in his language.

Dante couldn't understand a word of it. "What are you speaking?"

Deep creases appeared in his cheeks when he smiled and spoke in English again. "Sicilian. Better than Italian. No?"

Dante chuckled, not ready to get in the middle of that little battle. "What did you just say?"

"The food at the restaurant across the street is delicious."

"Is 'thank you' the same in both languages?" Lanelle asked.

Chapter 23

As they'd sat talking for the past twenty minutes, Lanelle prayed Dante would forget about her church fetish. If only she could've kept her reactions hidden. Which would've been the equivalent of asking Vanessa not to be snarky. She'd try for a little while, and then it would all get blown out the window.

Lanelle might've been a little hard on him when he'd disturbed her in the cathedral, but it seemed he could handle her tougher side. Couldn't he? At least he knew when to back off.

She twirled her fork in the succulent plate of spaghetti, making sure to capture a fresh clam. Damn, Italians—Sicilians, in this case—knew how to cook.

Slow down. Maybe breathe a little between bites. She paused in devouring the meal to chance a glance at Dante. If she hadn't swallowed the food in her mouth, she would've choked with her sharp intake of air. Did he know how sexy he was? Especially now, looking at her as if he wanted to eat her up instead of the veal Parmesan sitting on his plate.

Dante cut into his meat. "Can I ask you a question?"

She grabbed her water and took a sip to stall for time.

It helped her recover from the sudden dryness his query created. "Go ahead."

He placed the fork on his plate, giving her his complete attention. "I've observed you with Ryan and Vanessa. Disciplined and loving. You also speak to them with a respect that they appreciate. You'd make a fantastic mother."

She'd been thinking the same thing lately. Being with Ryan and Vanessa had made her maternal instincts and the longing to have children kick in. "Thank you."

He seemed to hesitate for a moment before speaking again. "I'm sorry for the loss of your children. No mother should have to bury a child."

He'd get no argument from her. The tight coiling of her stomach as Lanelle anticipated his next question threatened to bring up the food she'd just eaten.

"I was wondering…" He paused, clasped and unclasped his hands and wiped his brow before folding his hands together again. His uncharacteristic nervousness would've been endearing if he wasn't scaring her. "If you fell in love with someone who was Rh negative, would you be able and willing to have children with him?"

The man she loved had asked if she could physically have children. What if she gave him the wrong answer? Was he Rh negative? She reached for her glass only to find it empty. He handed her his untouched water and she took a huge gulp. "Why do you ask?"

"I'm interested in you," he said softly, as if he realized a sudden desire to bolt had come over her. "And even though I'm sure you won't admit to it, you like me, too."

Every inch of her skin heated as her heart rate quickened. *He likes me.* Tamping down her elation, she reminded herself of the negative aspect of the situation.

He filled in the silence when she didn't speak. "I thought we could talk about the possibility of starting a relationship. Was I wrong?"

Jumping up and running out on this forthright man would make her appear weak. Informing him that she wanted him more than her next breath would be too telling, so Lanelle took the middle ground. "We hardly know each other."

"What I know so far, I like. I want to learn more. If a relationship is too much for you right now, then how about friendship?" His lopsided grin brought a wicked glint to his eyes. "Maybe we can add in a few kisses, or a little more, to keep things interesting."

Oh, boy. "You've thrown me off guard with your candor." She sucked in a breath, then released it slowly in an attempt to get a grip on her emotions. She wanted to say yes, but she still wasn't ready. "Let's start with being friends."

"I can accept your decision." Dante's frown did everything to make her want to change her mind.

Every single cell in her body screamed to tell him her full name. Not to shake him off, but to release her from the guilt. And yet she couldn't tell him because he'd end up hating her for no real reason whatsoever. Maybe he'd be able to let go of this grudge he had and still like her for whom he'd come to know. Of course, lying to him, even by omission, was a pretty big deal.

"Good." Then she decided to admit the second thing that had the greatest potential of keeping him at bay for the rest of her life. "I can physically have children."

Before he could open his mouth, she rushed to say, "When I'm with you, I *feel* again. I haven't been attracted to anyone in years. I've kept my heart hidden and frozen. This made me happy because it meant I'd never have to deal with another man." She dropped her gaze. "And then you came along, making me laugh, cry and growl with anger. Breaking me out of the empty woman I'd turned into." Lanelle caught his gaze and shook her head. "I'm having difficulty handling it. The more I try to stay away, the closer we become, and that petrifies me."

He reached out a hand and clasped hers as he nodded. His strength infused her with the determination to proceed. "I know the one thing most people want more than anything is children. When you mentioned it at our first dinner together, I knew you did, too." She raised a shoulder, then let it drop.

"Yes, children are important, but I've realized life goes on without them." He jerked his head back. "Wait. That came out wrong. If the woman I end up with—" he paused as he stared into her eyes "—can't have children for whatever reason, then there are other ways."

When Lanelle didn't respond, he asked, "How do you feel now?"

The unexpected question slammed her back into her seat. *Other than a burning desire to make love to you? The overwhelming need to take care of you? Wanting to attempt to bear a child for you if we share blood compatibility?* "I like you." At least she'd been honest this time, rather than hiding behind a lie.

The corners of his lips lifted into a full-blown smile. "Was it so hard to say?"

If she'd summoned every ounce of courage stored within her, she would've told him her true feelings by waxing poetic about love. The emotion had snuck up on her like an insidious disease. Bit by bit, he'd wedged himself into her heart.

Dante had somehow dispelled the fear of disappointment instilled into her by her ex-husband's ready dismissal of their marriage. She was still more than her fair share of afraid, but he made her want to take the risk.

He withdrew his hand. "I did some research about rhesus factor."

Of course he did.

"Even if the RhoGAM never works, if you had a child with a rhesus-negative man, it wouldn't matter because the child would be negative and your cells wouldn't attack him or her."

She liked how he didn't call the baby "it." She nodded as she waited for him to continue.

"When I disappeared yesterday, I went to a lab and got tested. I'm negative. I knew my blood type was B-negative, but I never related it to the Rh factor before."

He waved a hand in front of her face as she sat unmoving, the news penetrating her brain. "Did you hear me?"

The fact that he'd gone to the trouble to find out said so much about how he felt about her. Could he be the man she'd waited all her life for? Lanelle swallowed and licked her lips. Now she felt really horrible about hiding her identity. Ready to admit the truth, she opened her mouth, only to have him place his fingers over them.

"You don't have to say anything now. I just wanted you to know."

Tell him. He'll forgive you.

As he called the waiter over for the check, the voice in her head kept getting fainter as the fear of losing him grew.

"Are you ready to head out?" he asked as he stood.

Her shoulders drooped as she realized how much of a coward she'd become. "Sure."

Back in the car, the tension within her made being with him uncomfortable. Following the directions of the gas attendant, they found themselves at the cable cars. Dante paid for a complete car so they'd be alone.

Deciding to enjoy the time she had with him, she let go of everything except her soaring heart when she realized just how much he cared about her. Since she felt the same, she knew things would work out. When the cable car started climbing, Lanelle wiggled her behind on the seat.

Dante raised his eyebrows. "What are you doing?"

"Checking to see if it'll shake. It's pretty stable."

"You'd be a nightmare to sit with on a Ferris wheel."

Lanelle laughed. "I take it you don't like when we try to flip it over?"

"Not at all."

They appreciated the scenery for the ten-minute ride. "It's breathtaking," Lanelle gushed as she snapped a photo. "Looking down on the town and the ocean is like a dream."

Dante felt the same way every time he saw Lanelle. He expected to wake up at any moment. *She likes me.* And yet she was still holding something back from him. He could sense it. The chicken in him wasn't ready to ask her about it, which disturbed him. The fact that he'd rather be with someone who withheld information rather than find out the truth wasn't like him at all.

Maybe if his heart weren't involved he'd make sure she told him her secret, but it was too late. Sitting at the restaurant looking into her eyes, he'd wanted her in his arms. Restaurant patrons be damned.

Taking it slow would be the best way to win her over. Long-term strategy over short-term pleasure.

Lanelle stiffened as his arms slid around her from behind. She looked over her shoulder to see that they were alone on the hilltop. With a wistful sigh, she leaned her back into his chest.

"You're more beautiful than the breathtaking scene before us," Dante whispered into her ear.

He turned her to face him and kissed her in that perfect moment. She clung to him as he reveled in the sweetness of her tender lips. Her smile didn't escape him when he groaned as she swept her tongue along his top lip. *Tease.* The grin disappeared as he delved his tongue into her mouth and swirled it around hers.

Stepping into Nirvana couldn't have been any better as she returned each stroke. Her fragrance, mixed with the barely discernible tangy smell of the ocean below as she clung to him, made the moment more poignant. He couldn't get enough of tasting her.

The giggles of a child sounded in his ears, making him pull away. Moving slowly toward what he imagined would be a beautiful relationship wouldn't do it for him. Not unless he wanted to take the risk of exploding whenever he was near her. "Will you stay with me here tonight?"

Her dark eyes searched his. Time ceased when she reached up and stroked his cheek. "Yes."

Chapter 24

Lanelle paced, or rather trudged, through the thick beige carpet of the extravagant suite Dante had booked after rushing them into the next available cable car back to Trapani. When the man wanted something, he went all out. Lanelle wiped her sweaty palms on her robe, thinking about how much he desired her.

His touches and stolen kisses at every stoplight on the drive to the hotel had kept her in a consistent state of longing. He'd left the room to make the pharmacy stop they'd both forgotten on their way over, and now apprehension clutched at her.

It didn't help that Lanelle could envision Cynthia's sly smile on the other end of the phone, even though Dante had been the one to tell his sister about them spending the night in Trapani when he'd borrowed her phone.

This isn't me. He hadn't promised her a future, only the night. Although the mention of a relationship at dinner implied more than just a fling.

He'd be the first man she'd slept with since her husband. *He'll see me naked.* The few stretch marks on her belly she'd earned from her pregnancies would soon be exposed. The ridiculous thoughts about her body ceased as the corner of her lip twitched, remembering how much he made her laugh.

They shared a connection. She'd felt it the first day they'd met. Knew it when the universe brought them together again at the fund-raiser. He brought out a passion in her that had lain dormant all her life.

She should tell him about her family. A sigh left her shoulders slumped over; she knew she wouldn't. Not tonight. The wall clock read four.

What was taking him so long? Maybe all the shops and pharmacies were closed.

She smacked her hands over her cheeks. She couldn't go through with it. How would she be able to face Vanessa and her family tomorrow? Lanelle moved to grab her clothes.

She jumped at the knock on the door just as she reached the small wardrobe where she'd folded her jeans and top.

The hesitancy in her steps made crossing the small room take forever. She sped up when the knock repeated. It could be only one person, but she asked, "Who is it?"

"Dante."

Unlocking the door, she swung it open and let him in. As he breezed past, her previous thoughts flittered away as her gaze caressed his strong back. Muscles she'd touched earlier flexed beneath his T-shirt as he placed the bag on a table in the corner of the room.

She'd have this night with him without regrets. The future might not exist for them, but tonight she'd quench the fire burning within her.

Turning, he approached her with open arms, and she leaped into them. Starting near her collarbone, he peppered a trail of kisses along her neck; when he reached her mouth, he plunged in. To her disappointment, he pulled back after too short a time.

He ran his hands over her back. "You smell fresh, like a garden."

She had an impossible time understanding what he'd said, although she'd watched his lips. "It's the bath soap." She forced her eyes to move to his. "They have quite the selection."

"Good." He nibbled her earlobe. "It's delectable on you, but I need a more masculine scent."

She grabbed the sides of his face, and the slight stubble of growth grazing her hands brought an increased sense of excitement. She pulled him down while rising onto her toes. If they had only tonight, she might as well set it off right.

Their lips fused as their tongues glided in a languorous manner. She slipped her hands around his back to draw him closer.

A moan escaped her when he opened her robe to rub his thumbs against her bare, hardened nipples.

She whimpered when the coolness of the air hit her lips as he ended the kiss.

"I want to take this slow. To be gentle." His ragged breath against her ear drove her further into a state of need.

Her glazed-over eyes attempted to focus. "Why?" She captured his mouth in another searing kiss, blocking any answer. There would be a time for sweetness, but right then she'd combust with her need to have him fill her. Love her.

Their kiss went wild as their hands roamed everywhere. They separated only long enough to strip his clothes and remove her robe. The pleasure of touching the tight, muscled body she'd admired for so long became an addiction.

When he tried to pull away, she refused to let go.

"I need to get a condom from the bag."

Lanelle dragged her hand along his waist as she moved behind him. They walked as one unit while she alternated between nipping, licking and sucking his back.

As he reached into the bag, his intake of breath as she reached around and rubbed the head of his erection made her feel deliciously naughty.

Pulling out a small box, he opened it to remove one of the condoms. She snatched it from his hand and stepped in front of him. She took a moment to appreciate his magnificence by stroking him before opening the packet. Loving the way his eyes closed and his head dropped back over his shoulders, she took her time slipping it on.

More than ready for him, she lifted herself onto the edge of the table and opened her legs, placing one on a nearby chair and curling the other around his hip. She'd never been this bold when it came to sex, but with Dante she seemed to know no other way.

Arching her back with her eyes closed, she anticipated he'd enter her immediately. When his hands stroked her thighs for a few seconds, she opened her eyes.

He gazed into her face.

"What?" Self-conscious under the scrutiny, she realized how wanton she must appear, splayed open for him.

"You are exquisite." He leaned forward and slid his lips over hers in a kiss so sweet it had no comparison. Then he increased the pressure. Her mouth opened, and he touched every crevice until she started sucking on his tongue. She moaned into his mouth when he reached between them to open her outer folds and touch her clit. He knew just how to stroke her as his fingers rubbed, bringing her close to climax.

The pressure became too much to contain as his fingers rotated faster while he thrust his tongue into her mouth. Lanelle let go, rasping his name as the spasms took over; collapsing onto his shoulder, she struggled to catch her breath.

He scooted her closer to the edge, lifted her legs over his forearms to widen them and stepped farther between. They stared at each other as he reached her entrance. The feeling of him filling and stretching her brought too much pleasure for her to maintain the eye contact. She closed her eyes, drowning in the sensations.

He stilled. "Look at me."

Forcing her lids open, she did as ordered, only to be rewarded when he thrust into her.

He set the rhythm. It didn't bother her that he had so much control over her body. She relinquished it without a qualm. Just as long as she could be one with him.

She experienced him everywhere. His scent filled her nose, his taste remained in her mouth, every inch of skin was aware of his touch. Most of all, he expanded her heart, which would burst at any moment.

Her nipples rubbed against his chest with each return stroke as he increased the pace, leading her into a tempo that would have her coming again. When he took her nipple into his mouth and sucked, she broke apart. Driving into her harder, Dante joined her, creating an intimacy the likes of which she'd never experienced.

Forever. The word drifted into her mind as she came down from the best sexual experience of her life. No matter what he chose to do, she'd be his until time stopped.

His heart rate slowed against her chest as they clung to each other. With the brush of his lips over her cheek, he eased out. The emptiness hit her more than the chill of the air conditioner on her damp skin.

He lifted her from the table and laid her on the bed, covering her with the sheet. His lingering lips brought a honeyed flutter into her belly.

Admiring his taut physique as he walked to the bathroom, she waited for his return. Would he cuddle with her? Would they talk? Or, like her ex-husband, would he stay alone and aloof on the other side of the bed?

Chapter 25

Dante crawled under the sheet and reached for his woman. There was no way he'd consider her anything less. She came willingly, snuggling against him with a sigh.

He smiled and brushed his chin against the top of her head. "Tell me about your dreams."

She lifted her head from his chest and frowned. Shifting their bodies a fraction, he kissed her. Her response urged him on. He released her lips with reluctance, finding it more important to hear her answer than to make love again. It would come soon enough.

He settled into the pillows. "Hasn't anyone asked you what your greatest desire in life is?"

"Never."

He squeezed her close. "I'm asking, so tell me."

The moments ticked by. "I don't have any. I stopped dreaming when my babies died."

"So there's nothing you long to do or have?" Dante refused to believe a person could go through life without a dream.

"You asked me why I like cathedrals so much." She drew in a breath and released it on a long warm exhale across his skin. "After losing the twins and my marriage,

I became inconsolable. I had no need to exist anymore, and I didn't want to."

Her voice was stronger than he expected it to be. "I went to counseling, but it didn't seem to be working. I lived in a state of depression. And I couldn't look at a baby without crying."

He caressed a hand down her arm. Solid and soft.

"I wanted to die."

Dante stifled the panic that rose. "But you didn't."

The shift of her cheek tickled his chest when she smiled. "Unless you just had sex with a ghost."

"Stranger things have happened, although not to me. Tell me more."

"My mother, lost as to how to help me, led me to a church a couple of months later. Not our normal one, but a cathedral I'd never set foot in. The message the priest gave brought tears to my eyes. He spoke about forgiveness and learning to move forward. Existing in the pain would help no one, especially the person suffering. It was as if I'd been delivered there for those words."

She lifted her torso and braced a forearm on his chest. He missed the contact of her body flush against his. Looking into her eyes made up for it.

"When the service ended, we stayed seated, allowing the priest's words to echo in my head. As if some kind of miracle had descended on me, all of a sudden I had a reason to live. I realized I couldn't live *for* anyone. Life is for me." She nodded as if reaffirming what she'd learned. "With my mother by my side, not having said a word the entire time, I stood and meandered through every area of the building, appreciating the statues and stained glass windows. Touching the pews as if they held a life of their own. I finally saw the beauty of being alive, even if my children hadn't been able to make it."

He didn't have to imagine her reverence in the church; he'd witnessed it firsthand.

"I lost track of time as we wandered. The priest asked if there was a problem. I'll never forget the compassion that filled his eyes when I broke down and told him everything, ending with how much his words had touched me. He must've been a busy man, but he took the time to listen and console me. Do you know what Father Patrick did next?"

Dante shook his head, not having a clue.

"He prayed for me and told me to return the next day."

"I take it you went back."

"I couldn't stay away. When I was younger, I wanted to be a nun, but once I left Catholic school I realized it wasn't for me. Maybe it wasn't too late."

"Did I just sleep with a reverend sister?"

Lanelle smacked his shoulder with a giggle. "No. I didn't become a nun."

Dante believed there were no coincidences in life. Destiny had a way of making things happen so it would be fulfilled. "So what happened?"

"Father Patrick had me volunteer at a women's shelter. My life changed from there. These women had gone through much worse than me, and yet they'd survived and continued to try to make a better life for themselves and their children. Father Patrick reminded me I had a purpose in life and I had to fulfill it." Her eyes shone.

"I'd like to meet this man and thank him for helping you."

She rested her head on his chest. "He got transferred to Tennessee, but we still keep in contact. He ended up being a true friend and mentor."

"Then we'll go visit him." He'd committed himself and looked forward to the trip one day.

"What for?"

Because he saved the life of the woman I love fell short of slipping out of his mouth. He didn't think she'd be able to handle something he'd barely gotten a grasp on. "Because he helped you and brought you back to life."

"I gave an anonymous donation to Father Patrick's church. I didn't tell them what to do with the money, but they ended up expanding the shelter. Even though he left, it still thrives, and I donate to help keep it running."

Humbled by the woman in his arms, he inhaled their mingled scents as he squeezed her.

They lay silent for a long time. Just when he thought she'd fallen asleep, she whispered, "My dream is to be a mother."

"Then we'll work on making it happen." Feeling the stirring of desire, he rolled her onto her back. "Just call me the dream maker." He had no doubt one day they'd have a child, whether biologically or by other means. But tonight, he'd focus on pleasure.

Chapter 26

On the way back to Agrigento the next afternoon, Lanelle snuck a peek at Dante as he drove.

Being with him had been amazing. She leaned her head against the seat and closed her eyes. Recalling each caress and whisper they'd shared brought a prickle of heat to her skin.

He grabbed her hand. "You're smiling."

Intertwining their fingers, she looked at him. "So are you. I was remembering."

"Those must be some damn good memories."

"Indeed." Dante's words of making her dream come true rose up to taunt her. She wanted him to be the father of her child. For the first time in years, she was willing to endure whatever pain might come along with creating a baby.

He couldn't have meant what he'd promised. *He still doesn't know my true identity. What will he say when I tell him?* The image of sparks flying from his body from pure rage filled her imagination.

"What excuse did you give the others about why we spent the night in Trapani?" Lanelle asked in order to divert her attention from the unintended subterfuge, which could break them up before they had a chance to solidify what they shared.

"My sister didn't ask." He turned to her and wiggled his brows. "I figure they already knew I wanted a night of nooky with you."

"Cut it out. They won't think we had sex, will they?"

"The way you're glowing, they'll have no doubt."

She pulled the visor down to look in the mirror. Nothing had changed, except that she couldn't get rid of the silly grin. "I'm not glowing."

"Maybe I'm overlaying the memory of you calling my name with your orgasm this morning." He looked at her for a moment before returning his attention to the road. "We need to change the topic. I'm thinking of pulling over."

Lanelle hoped her sidelong glance came out saucy. "I wouldn't mind stopping."

He groaned and squeezed her hand. "Don't tempt me, love."

Love. There it was again. He'd whispered it as they'd made love last night. It wasn't anything more than a simple term of endearment.

The exhaustion from the night of lovemaking, mixed with too little sleep, caught up to her. On her way to drifting off, she murmured, "Hmm?" when Dante called her name.

"Last night you mentioned donating money to the shelter Father Patrick ran."

Her eyes sprang open. She'd been so involved with her experience of the past, she'd forgotten about exposing herself. "Yes."

"Who are you?"

Playing dumb would insult his intelligence and draw out his anger. He'd made it more than clear he detested lying. Why would she risk not having him fall in love with her over a tiny nondisclosure? Besides, he had money, power and confidence of his own. He didn't need hers.

Those things can never be enough. People always seek more. Lanelle hushed her inner cynic. Or was it her inner realist? Either way, she'd tell him everything. "My name is—"

"Lanelle Murphy. I know. What I'm looking for is how you were able to give the shelter so much money. Expansions to a facility aren't cheap."

She dived into her bag when her cell started ringing. Postponing the inevitable for a couple of more minutes couldn't hurt anything. The annoyance on Dante's face claimed otherwise.

Brad's number flashed on the phone. "Can you please pull over? I have to take this call."

"I'm driving, not you."

She cut her eyes at him. As she answered, Dante pulled the car to the side of the road, and she hopped out.

Knowing it wasn't a social call, she got to the point. "What's up, Brad?"

"I finished my run-through of the NICU." His pause didn't bode well. "Lanelle, someone cut so many corners the place is on the cusp of being dangerous to anyone who walks in."

Her stomach bottomed out.

"The materials used were below substandard, covered over to make people think they were of superior quality. And whoever constructed it only considered the bottom line."

Anger raced through her. All she'd wanted to do was provide a place of healing for premature babies. Someone had put people at risk with their greed. "Will it need to be torn down?"

"The foundation is actually solid, so it could be worse."

She scoffed. "It could be better."

"True."

Trusting her friend as she did one of her own brothers, she asked, "So what's the way forward?"

"Get in touch with the hospital's project manager and have them call off the workers who are there. They'd only be wasting their time at this point. When you get back, you'll need to have a major meeting with the board to see how to progress. Has your accountant been able to find anything in the books?"

She shook her head. "Not yet. Can you please do me another favor?"

He chuckled. "Since you rarely ask for anything, sure, I'll go through the construction bids and see if I spot something shady."

"I owe you."

"No, you don't."

"Thanks, Brad."

"Other than calling off the flooring people, there's nothing you need to do. So enjoy the rest of the vacation."

Worried sick, she knew the impossibility of such an order. "We leave tomorrow, so I'll be back soon."

A brief goodbye from both sides and the line went dead.

Head down in extreme distress, Lanelle turned and caught Dante watching her, and once again her courage failed. She couldn't tell him. She just couldn't. After looking up the project manager on her phone, she called and told him to contact Calvano Flooring to inform them to halt work on the project.

The calls to the board could wait until she got back to the hotel.

Lanelle trundled to the car to face her shame. She might as well try to enjoy the last day she had with him. Once he found out about her being an Astacio and her involvement in the project, whatever he may have started to feel for her would disappear into the ether.

Dante met her at the passenger side door. "Is everything okay?"

Squaring her shoulders, she told him the truth. "It will be. I just have a rat to catch."

"Want to talk about it?"

"Thanks, but I need to process it all first."

He rubbed his hands along her arms, then pulled her in for a hug—the one thing she'd wanted most at that point. But with all her deception and spinelessness, she didn't deserve it, so she pushed away and forced a smile up at him before sitting in the car.

He'd receive the news about the NICU soon. Would she be able to complete it? Brad seemed optimistic. How would it affect Dante's chances of expanding his business and keeping control of his company?

Not for the first time, she wished she'd been better able to keep an eye on the business dealings of the project during its most critical phase.

Shake it off. What's done is done. Time to move forward.

The rest of the ride back had consisted of two hours of silent torment. Dante had tried several times to reach out to Lanelle during the interminable trip. He didn't like the fact that she'd recoiled into herself and decided to stay there rather than share what had happened.

It made him realize how much he didn't know about her. Was this how she solved all of her problems? Alone? The thought of not being needed dismayed him.

Dante returned the NICU project site manager's emergency call once he'd found his phone sitting on the desk of his hotel room and checked his messages. One of the best workers Dante had ever known wouldn't have called him, knowing he was on vacation, for anything trivial. "What's going on, Alex?"

"How's Italy?"

"What did you want to talk to me about?"

Alex chuckled. "A little small talk won't kill you. Besides everything's fine now, mostly. We have two issues. Philip fell through one of the interior walls. The drywall they used was more like paper, so when he leaned on it, it crumbled. He landed so hard, he dislocated his shoulder. It could've been much worse. As always, he followed protocol and wore a hard hat. We got everyone out of there so fast we were all a blur."

Dante's heart continued its acceleration. "How's Philip?"

"The doctor ordered him not to do any heavy lifting for two weeks after popping the shoulder back in. No concussion or other injury."

"If there had been patients in there…"

Alex clicked his tongue. "A baby or more, depending on the setup, would've died under his weight. I'd hate to think how many other shortcuts they took during construction. I wouldn't be surprised if the whole building caved in. But our floors would remain intact. No doubt about it."

Dante could barely contain his rage as he squeezed the phone so hard it hurt his hand. Whoever the hospital contracted to do the work used cheap materials, but to put people's lives at risk by not following the basic rules of construction spoke of pure irresponsibility. He detested Eliana Astacio for not caring enough to do the right thing when it came to her *beloved* project. He bet her home wasn't crumbling around her. "When did it happen?"

"A couple of hours ago."

While he'd been trying to figure out how to get Lanelle out of her funk, his workers' lives had been in jeopardy. "What's going on now?" Dante gritted out. Again angry at himself that he'd forgotten his phone. *What could I have done about it other than cuss up a storm earlier?*

"I sent the crew home. And then a call came from the hospital, telling me they couldn't reach you. They're suspending the project."

Dante snorted. "Did they know about Philip getting injured?"

"I hadn't told anyone. Maybe they realized what a crap job they'd done."

"Any media involvement?"

"None I'm aware of. I'm pretty sure the hospital will want to keep it low-key."

"You've done a good job, Alex," Dante praised, as guilt for not reporting the shoddy workmanship when he'd first discovered it ate at his gut. "Thanks for keeping me updated."

"Sure thing."

Dante disconnected the call. Stifling a roar, he swiped a hand down his face. A punch to the wall would only end up breaking his hand. Why the hell would anyone take such a chance on people's lives?

He made a quick call to Philip to verify his condition and then to the hospital administrator with whom he'd been in contact when he'd gotten the bid. No answer. No big surprise. His ass was probably on fire.

Dante could choke someone, preferably Astacio, who had approved this nonsense, but whom would it help? At least nobody had been seriously hurt, especially an innocent baby fighting for her life.

What would happen to the project? Obviously, they'd have to redo the walls, maybe the whole wing. How long would this hold up construction on the floors and his workers' time? Other projects sat in the wings, ready to be started. He wouldn't even think about how it would affect his expansion and the effect on his profit margin.

There was nothing he could do about it at this point.

The stress of the job could be held off for a couple of more days. He'd be flying back tomorrow anyway; he might as well enjoy the rest of the vacation. Or at least try.

Chapter 27

Lanelle had taken a walk on the beach to clear her head and think out solutions to the mess she'd gotten herself in with both Dante and the hospital.

Lanelle checked the cell phone messages she'd received. One from the secretary of the board calling an emergency meeting that afternoon tied her stomach in knots. Rather than panic, she called her only friend on the board: Hubert, a general member like her who shared similar suspicions about the project and the missing money.

"Hi, Hubert, I got a message about the meeting. Unfortunately, I'm on vacation in Italy and can't make it. What's going on?"

"One of the flooring contractors fell through a wall."

Lanelle's body tensed at the same time as her knees weakened, and she slammed her behind into the chair. "Oh, my goodness. Is he all right?"

"Yes, from what I've heard, but everyone's in a panic. If it had occurred when filled with babies, someone could've gotten killed."

Fuming, she jumped out of her seat and stomped across the floor. Never had she imagined something bad would come from one of her ventures. The thought of an innocent life being destroyed because of her work made her swallow back the bile crawling up her throat.

Lanelle attempted to stay rational. Maybe if she'd told Dante to haul his people out of the project when she'd first heard the news, then the guy wouldn't have gotten hurt. Her head throbbed with the guilt of her cowardice.

"I'll call Reginald and have him link me into the meeting via teleconferencing."

"Sounds like a plan. I'll see you later, then."

"Bye."

Taking a moment to release some of the tension before speaking to the president of the board, Lanelle downed a bottle of water. That's when it hit her. Dante would be hunting down Eliana Astacio. No time to analyze how much more he'd hate her or how she'd lost any chance of ever being with him.

She made the call to the board president, arranging her involvement in the meeting. As soon as she finished, a knock sounded on the door. She looked through the peephole to see Dante pacing in the hallway. Her first reaction was to ignore the summons and slip out of Sicily like some kind of thief in the night. A mental slap cured her of the ridiculous idea.

As a distant descendant of the kings of Spain, albeit through a more illegitimate side of the family, she had a duty of pride and honor to sustain the Astacio name. Every one of her father's Spanish ancestors had probably turned over in his or her grave at how she'd denied who she was to a man she claimed to love.

Opening the door, she stepped back as he rushed in. Obviously he'd heard about what happened at the hospital.

"Remember I told you about the NICU project my company is working on?"

Lanelle swallowed hard and nodded.

"I told you the contractor had used inferior products,

but I didn't think anyone would get hurt. One of my crew members fell through a wall." He brushed his hands over his pants, then flexed his fingers. "A wall!" he exclaimed. "Do you know how cheap the bastard would have to be to use substandard drywall?" Seemingly spent, he sat on the bed, propped his elbows on his knees and held his head. "What if a baby had been in there? One thing I never sacrifice with my work or my staff is safety. Nobody should die because of inferior quality."

"I agree. Dante..." How could she tell him?

He looked at her with slits for eyes as his jaw clenched and unclenched repeatedly before exclaiming with a fist in the air, "If I ever get my hands on Eliana Astacio..."

Lanelle stepped back, a true fear now residing in her chest. He wouldn't hurt her physically, but words could be just as damaging. She'd lost him even before she knew the greatness she'd found in having such a man at her side. Time to face the consequences of her lies. "The NICU is my project."

He sprang to his feet, his brow furrowed. "Your contractors did the work?"

"No. Hell, no." If it had been up to her, she would've chosen Brad to construct the wing. None of this would've been an issue. "I'm a board member. I came up with the idea for the new NICU. I even donated millions to ensure it happened. Unfortunately, I was tied up with a pressing issue with my father's company. The whole family had been called in to deal with a crisis that my father couldn't trust anyone else to deal with, so I had no involvement with who got chosen for the bids."

The tension in the room built as she swallowed. "All I wanted was to build a high-tech facility to provide wonderful care for premature babies." She sighed, recalling her own innocent children. "All in memory of the ones I lost. Who knew someone would take it and twist it around?"

His voice came out gravelly. "Did you say the project is yours?"

Lanelle nodded.

He took three steps backward, only to bump into the wall. "You." His eyes went wide as he repeated the question he'd asked in the car. "Who are you?"

The moment of truth had arrived, and yet she still didn't want to face it. "I never meant to lie to you. At first I didn't think you needed to know. I've lived my life as Lanelle Murphy, previously Gill, to protect me from being hounded by the press."

"Who are you?"

At his raised voice, she jumped. "It's kept me safe all these years. And then you had this prejudice, and I didn't think anything would happen between us. But then I wanted to tell you last night, but I got—" her voice lowered "—scared. I swear I was going to tell you in the car."

His growl prompted her to rush out, "My full name is Eliana Lanelle Gill Astacio Murphy."

The anger he resonated stood at complete odds with the smile that had appeared on his face. She ignored both and looked into his eyes. A pain so deep she felt it in her belly resided there. What had she done?

"I can't believe this," he said to himself more than to her. "Of all the people on earth I could've fallen in—" Her gasp stopped him midsentence. And then he looked at her—no, *through* her. "It had to be a liar."

She had it coming. "Dante, I'm sorry."

He snapped up a hand. "Now you know why I hate your people so much. You're so selfish that even thinking about others goes beyond your concept of reality. Sure, you give money to charities, but those are faceless, nameless schmucks you don't have to interact with. You don't get your hands dirty like the rest of us." He hauled in a deep breath. "And you certainly don't have true relationships with the common folk, either."

Now livid, no longer at just herself, she came to her own defense. "Your singular experience with your spoiled ex-fiancée," she spat out, "has biased you, and I won't let you apply it to me."

He poked a finger into his chest. "Are you blaming all of this on me?"

Shrinking into herself a little, she realized how wrong she'd been.

Before she could respond, he raised a brow in a much too condescending manner. "What are you going to do, Ms. Astacio?" Her last name came out with so much contempt she winced. "Call me a liar? Oh, wait. That's you, isn't it? A coward, a liar and a dirty dealer."

She'd rather contend with his yelling than his disappointment at her actions. When he stomped toward the door, panic claimed her and she gripped his arm. He wrenched it out of her grasp. "Please, Dante. I'm sorry," she sobbed. "About everything."

After opening the door, he froze, then he turned to look at her with his eyes bright, as if another idea had manifested. "The phone call in the car, who was it from?"

Dammit. Couldn't she catch a break? She backed away, no longer able to anticipate how he'd react. "It was Brad. After you told me about the inferior material they'd used on-site, I had him do an inspection of it. He gave me the results today."

He slammed the door so hard when he stepped back in that it sprang open. "You knew and you didn't tell me to get my workers out of the decayed piece of garbage you call a building?"

She swallowed her fear. "I contacted the project manager to inform you." The explanation sounded lame even to her ears.

"So Philip falling through a wall rests on your shoulders. Both as Eliana Astacio and Lanelle Murphy. You two really are one in the same. Self-centered to the core."

She had no response as his eyes shot daggers at her. She'd been too wrapped up in her own fear of how he'd react to the news to even contemplate something bad happening at the site. Her apology came too late, but she still had to get it out. "I know you won't believe me, but I'm sorry. For everything. I'll do my best to rectify the situation."

He waved a hand between them. "As for you and me, it's too late. But I know you'd better damn well do something good about the NICU. It was a worthy project. Too bad someone better couldn't have done the job."

He stormed out of her room, leaving nothing behind but the soft click of the door closing as her heart proceeded to shatter.

She squared her shoulders and let the Astacio sense of duty fill her. "No time to break down. I have work to do." The first thing on her list was to let her parents know the extent of the mess she'd gotten herself into. Second would be her accountant to see if he'd come up with any answers to the procurement fraud with the forensic accountant and Brad's help.

The last call would be to the most difficult person to deal with in the world: her brother Leonardo. Of course he'd rub her face in the situation, but he'd help her. He might not be the nicest person to deal with, but he was damn good at his job, and corporate law suited him. She had a feeling that before the mud cleared, she'd need his services more than anyone else's.

As for Dante, she'd had her chance and lost him. She'd cry over him later. After all, she had the rest of her life to live without him.

Chapter 28

Her escape to Italy had been the best time of Lanelle's life, up until it all got shot down into the pits of hell. Two weeks had passed since she'd landed on American soil, and she hadn't stopped running since. The busy nature of the meetings hadn't allowed her to miss Dante as much. At least, not until she got home in the evenings and memories of him overwhelmed her. That's when she'd crumble into a ball of snot and tears, knowing she'd never love another man as she had him.

Another night of misery awaited her as she stepped into her apartment. At least this time the day had been filled with excellent news. She tossed a newspaper onto the coffee table, kicked off her heels and flopped onto the couch. The headline made her angry and happy at the same time: Six Caught in Procurement Scandal at Livingstone Hospital.

What the article didn't state was who the team consisted of. Two of the bastards were on the board. One of them owned the construction company that had built the wing. Motivated by greed, they'd stolen from a project from which maybe one of their own family members or friends may have one day benefited. Toshia had been right:

no matter how much a person had, some always wanted more and would do anything to get it.

The camera-shy Eliana Astacio and her need for justice were mentioned in the article as playing a key role in discovering the fraudulent activities. Would they be able to retrieve all of the stolen money? Unfortunately no, but Lanelle was happy they'd get the majority of it back.

She'd make sure the companies that had done such shoddy work on her project never built anything else in Ohio again. If she had the power to extend the blackball beyond her home state, she would.

She rubbed her chest to abate the pain that had taken up permanent residence over the past two weeks. Using what energy remained, she got up and went to the kitchen. Triple chocolate chip cookie dough ice cream had definitive healing properties, but she couldn't sustain such therapy without fat-inducing consequences for too much longer. How could she remedy what she'd done to Dante?

She jerked her head up at the rattle of keys. Other than her, only Toshia had a set.

Her best friend spoke before she'd crossed the threshold. "I'm tired of you being too busy to stop by my place or hang out."

Lanelle ignored her and switched the channel.

Toshia shoved Lanelle's feet off the couch. "You left me for two weeks, sending me some flimsy postcard and one phone call, sounding happy as hell. And then you come back running all over Cleveland, making absolutely no time for *me*. What the hell is going on?"

"Italy—"

"I've been there. Gorgeous landscape and people, and *the* most delicious food." Toshia assessed Lanelle from head to toe. "Judging from your chunkier stature, which looks good on you, I'm sure you can attest to the food.

What I want to know is what happened with the hot piece of dark chocolate who footed the bill."

It didn't take much to call forth a blasé tone. Her excitement over Dante had diminished, knowing she'd messed up. "I fell in love with him, we had sex, I almost got one of his workers killed and when I told him I was Eliana—" she ate a spoonful of the ice cream and spoke around it "—let's just say I deservedly got chewed out and he left me."

Toshia sat on the couch and patted Lanelle on the head. "You know I don't do outlines. Give me more details. By the way, congrats on nailing the assholes who were stealing from the hospital. Eliana came off as one kick-ass righter-of-wrongs."

Lanelle gave the most genuine smile she'd been able to deliver all day. There was nothing like a best friend to know what she needed. She explained everything that had happened in Italy.

At the end of the telling, Lanelle felt better. Still without Dante, but it was good to discuss it. A quick analysis of Toshia as she made her way to the kitchen had Lanelle changing the subject. "Why does your ass look so big?"

"I'm getting fat like you?"

Lanelle leaped up and ran to her friend. Her belly was bulging a little, too. "Oh, my goodness! You're pregnant." Lanelle gathered Toshia into a tight hug. "How far along?"

Toshia swatted Lanelle's hand when she placed a palm on her belly. "You aren't upset?"

Lanelle could ring her friend's neck. She'd been hiding her joy because of her? Once again she clung to Toshia. "I'm so happy for you I could *Riverdance* all over this house."

"Please don't."

Lanelle tugged her to the dark mahogany dining room set and pulled out two chairs. "How many months?"

The slightest twinge of jealousy rushed into her when

Toshia rubbed her belly. She had no right to be anything but happy for her friend.

"Six months."

"But you're so small."

"I know, right? My mother said, with my eldest sister, she barely showed at eight months. By the time she got down to me, she claimed her belly was so big she couldn't fit through doors when she tried to pass sideways."

Lanelle laughed.

Toshia gestured to the bump. "I didn't know how you'd take it, so I kept putting off telling you."

"You stuck by me through the hardest part of my life. Why wouldn't I celebrate with you?"

"Because it's a reminder of what you lost."

The memory of Dante's scent after making love slammed into her. "Do you know what he promised me?"

"What?"

"I don't know why, but when I was with him, the fear of having a baby diminished. I could see myself pregnant with his child." She rubbed Toshia's belly. "I told him my dream was to be a mother, and he said he'd make it come true."

Toshia's sniffles foreshadowed her tears. "He did not."

"And I believed him. Right before I lost him."

Toshia rolled her eyes and got up. "I'm hungry for some cake. Do you have any?"

Confused at the attitude, Lanelle spun her around. "What?"

"Sometimes you can be too dramatic to bear."

"Me? Me?" Lanelle poked the center of her chest. "Did I hold up a mirror? Me?"

"There you go." Toshia headed into the kitchen and smiled when she saw the half-eaten German chocolate layer cake under the glass holder. "I knew you wouldn't disappoint."

Lanelle wouldn't get any more information from Toshia until she fed her. Recalling how those hunger pangs had driven her crazy, she rushed to get things set. Nothing had satisfied her except what she'd desired. While Toshia grabbed two glasses and a carton of milk, Lanelle retrieved plates and a knife. She placed a slice on one.

Toshia pointed to the piece of cake. "I hope that's for you because it's way too small for me and this little munchkin."

Lanelle laughed and doubled the size of the next piece. "Better?"

"Much."

In the living room, she allowed Toshia to appease herself with the cake before going on the attack about her earlier reaction. "Okay, now tell me what you meant."

"Did Dante say he didn't want to be with you?"

"He told me it was too late for us. Plus, he hasn't tried to contact me. I returned on an earlier flight than them, so I haven't seen him since Italy." She sighed. "I called Vanessa to make sure they arrived safely and she told me how sullenly Dante had behaved on the way back home. We've spoken a few times since then, but the topic of Dante never comes up." She didn't need Vanessa to be stuck in the middle of their mess.

Toshia regarded her. "To be honest, I think you did the right thing not telling him."

Lanelle blinked. "You do?"

"We'd been inseparable at school for three years before you told me. How long had you known Dante? You weren't sure if you could even trust him. The paparazzi would probably pay millions for a picture of the elusive Eliana Astacio. Isn't that why you make the members of every board you sit on sign a nondisclosure agreement?"

"But I was still wrong."

Toshia put the empty plate down. "Yeah, you should've told him once you realized you could trust him. But…"

"But what?"

"You have to admit his reason for not liking you before he even knew who you were was ridiculous. Just because one rich chick bails doesn't mean everyone will."

"I told him the same thing. So what should I do?"

"Other than finding out who his ex is and kicking her behind?"

The thought had run through Lanelle's mind more than once. "Something that wouldn't end up with Leonardo having to represent me in criminal court would be better."

"I'm not one to give advice—"

Lanelle snorted.

"—but I'd call him and apologize again."

"Do you think it'll work?"

Toshia shrugged as she reached for Lanelle's plateful of cake. "I'm not psychic. You'll just have to try it and see. If he doesn't accept your apology, then he's a jerk of magnum proportions and doesn't deserve the wonderfulness of you."

She didn't know about all that, but she hoped the time they'd spent apart had been as miserable for him as it had been for her, making him ready to forgive and forget.

Lanelle felt better with a plan in place. Now, time to focus on her best friend. "Tell me how you've been feeling. Any changes?"

"I found a damn stretch mark on my belly." She rubbed her abdomen. "I cocoa buttered the bitch up."

Lanelle relaxed as Toshia entertained her, putting Dante out of her mind. At least for a short while.

Chapter 29

The smell of his sister's irresistible gumbo had Dante's stomach grumbling for the first time in over two weeks. These days he ate solely for sustenance, not for enjoyment as they'd done in Italy.

Cynthia stirred the contents of the pot. "So when are you going to get off your high horse and call Lanelle?"

"Yeah, Uncle D," Vanessa supported her mother. "Did you hear she took down an embezzlement scam that's been happening for years? I still can't believe we know an Astacio. Miguel is so hot. I wonder if Lanelle will introduce him to me."

Cynthia pointed the spoon at her daughter. "You aren't going anywhere near that playboy. And remember, you promised not to tell a soul."

"How about her older brother? He's a lawyer. Can I meet him?"

"Vanessa," Cynthia growled.

"Fine, Mom. The only Astacio I'll hang out with is Lanelle." She glared at Dante. "If she'll still be my friend."

Dante had nothing to say on the matter. Vanessa could be friends with whomever she wanted. He'd prefer liars be excluded. He'd stayed away from his sister's home so he wouldn't be harassed about Lanelle. It helped that he'd had to play catch-up at work with back-to-back meetings.

Cynthia sat at the table adjacent to him. "You know I never liked your ex, Martha. She was always so stuck-up and hoity when I came to visit you on campus. And I know she didn't like me, either, but she'd play pretend when you were around."

They'd had this conversation years ago when his ex-fiancée had dumped him.

His sister shook her head. "It's not my job to convince you of anything—your heart should be taking care of that. All I know is I've never seen you as happy with a woman as you were with Lanelle. She's the same woman you fell in love—" She held up her hand to stop him from speaking. "Don't you dare lie to me."

"You mean, like she did to me?"

Cynthia waved down a hand. "She went into self-preservation mode. People like Vanessa would be all over her if they knew her real identity."

Vanessa sat up straight in protest. "Hey."

Her mother ignored her. "Tell me you didn't honestly expect her to tell a virtual stranger when they first meet you that she's an heiress when she's kept herself hidden from the world for years."

"I've thought about it, but how can I forgive her for putting my workers in danger when she could've just told me the truth?"

Cynthia placed a hand on her hip as she glowered at him. "If you hadn't talked about her to her face, maybe she wouldn't have felt so intimidated to tell you directly."

The air he blew through his lips caused them to vibrate. "She's fearless. Afraid of nothing."

Cynthia stood. "Except losing you. Love will make a person do some pretty messed-up things." When she went back to the stove, Dante knew lecture time had finished.

Vanessa nodded as if she'd experienced it all before. "I remember what you told me when I was going through chemo. The things you want, you will fight for."

"And then you vomited all over my brand-new loafers."

She chuckled. "Chemo was horrific, but that was funny. She's special, and you know it. Please don't let her go, Uncle D."

The spare moments he'd had over the past couple of weeks had been spent contemplating and remembering Lanelle. His pride had been beaten and fried over the fact that she'd been able to deceive him. And yet he was a little embarrassed he'd actually put Eliana down, even though he'd never met her.

He took a deep breath, and the aromatic, spice-laden air filled his lungs. He loved Lanelle. He always would. Not for the first time, he wondered if he'd be able to forgive her.

Interrupted by her doorbell during the six o'clock news, Lanelle plodded to the entryway in her hot-pink fuzzy slippers. She wasn't expecting anyone, and Toshia would've barged in again using her key. Nobody stood at the entrance of the peephole. She lowered her voice to make it sound more masculine. "Who is it?"

He stepped into the scope of the peephole, and her breath caught at the warped sight of him. "It's me. Dante."

What was he doing here? She'd called him a few times yesterday, with the call going to voice mail. The fourth time, she'd left a message apologizing once again for having deceived him and endangering his workers.

When she hadn't heard back, she figured she'd blown any chance she'd ever had with him.

Admonishing the butterflies in her stomach to settle down didn't help. She glanced down at her unattractive, old, faded, stretched-out jogging suit and calculated how long it would take to dash to her room and change. Way too long. She opened the door. A sweep of her hand indicated he should enter.

He moved into her foyer, pivoted in her direction and passed a hand over his head. He looked as tired as she felt, with dark circles under his eyes. His designer suit hung a little loose on him. Her heart lurched, knowing that she'd caused him so much pain. She pushed down the lump in her throat. "Let's go have a seat."

His stare kept her immobile. "What does your family call you?"

It took her a moment to understand the question. "Depends on who you talk to and when. But mostly they call me El."

He nodded. "It could work for either name. Which do you prefer?"

"From your lips? Lanelle."

He winced at the slight reminder of how he'd spoken about Eliana. "I got your message. I'm sorry I couldn't call back."

Hurt that he didn't bother to explain why, she lowered her gaze to her slippers and waited for him to get to the point of his visit so she could curl up on the couch and cry.

"Eliana Astacio," he said softly.

She lifted her head.

"I'm sorry I offended you. I had no idea you were this gracious, passionate, loving, funny, adventurous woman. I made a mistake. I based my opinion of you on a prior relationship with a woman of your similar social standing who hurt me. I was a fool to do so."

Lanelle wiped the tears from her eyes with the sleeve of her top and swallowed hard.

"Lanelle Murphy," he said, once again in a reverent tone. "I am truly sorry for being selfish and expecting you to tell me right away that you were Eliana, especially when

I showed such disrespect toward a woman whose father I'd worked with and liked. You had every right to protect yourself from people who may have wanted to do harm. I believe you when you said you were going to tell me."

Her heart mended with every word. She'd chosen the right man to love, even if he might not want her anymore.

He broke eye contact to look into the mirror that hung to his left. After a moment he returned his gaze. "I'm still upset that you didn't trust me enough to tell me that my workers were in trouble, but I can understand why you did. You thought I would hate you because I detested who I thought Eliana was."

Lanelle shook her head. "It's no excuse. I regret that moment of cowardice. I'm so sorry."

He pointed between them. "Other than what would've happened between us, you telling me wouldn't have mattered. My worker fell through the wall a couple of hours before Brad did the inspection."

A sob of relief escaped. It wasn't her fault. She'd always feel ashamed for not acting when she should've. "I'll never be such a coward again. Never put my fear over doing the right thing. I promise."

He smiled. "I believe you. Whatever you set your mind to, you achieve. All a person has to do is read any kind of media to see how you stomped down those project embezzlers. You are one powerful woman."

Lanelle nodded once and waited. Would they be able to be together?

"Eliana Lanelle Gill Astacio." He hung his head. "I was no better than the asshole ex-husband who abandoned you."

She would've rushed to him in denial, but she didn't know how he'd react. "You were justified in your anger. I was in the wrong, too."

"But I shouldn't have closed you out. That was my greatest mistake and I will always regret it."

A huge weight lifted off her shoulders. At least now, if they couldn't be together as lovers, they could sustain their friendship. "I forgive you, Dante."

"El," he said with a small smile. "I've missed you so much. I felt as if my heart was torn from my chest and shoved back in. Will you please take me back?"

She couldn't help the smile spreading across her face. "Yes. I missed you, too, Dante."

He swung her into his arms and landed a hard kiss on her mouth. Easing the tension, he teased her lips. Her body responded by returning the caresses and grasping his shoulders. She never wanted to be away from him again.

When he pulled his head back, she followed, refusing to let the kiss end. This time their tongues met. She relaxed, his cologne and hard body making her melt into him.

Desire took over as he deepened the kiss, sweeping his tongue inside the crevices of her mouth. Him naked and filling her became her only priority.

He wrenched his mouth away. "I've missed you so much." He peppered kisses over her face in between the words.

With an audacity she'd found the courage to exhibit only with him, she purred, "Then show me."

"Which way to your bedroom?"

"It's upstairs." She nuzzled his neck, then clasped onto his hand and rushed into the living room. "Much too far away. The sofa will do for now."

Dante's hand roamed over Lanelle's abdomen. He held it still at her giggle.

"I thought my loving would've been enough to make you sleep," he teased.

"Considering I did all the work, I should be tired."

Tilting her chin, he rubbed the tip of her nose with his. "I helped a little."

"If you say so." She snuggled into him.

Dante rolled her onto her back and tickled her.

"You helped. You did," she relented in between giggles.

He picked up the blanket from the floor and repositioned it to cover them, then wrapped his arm around her as they spooned. Life couldn't get any better.

"What's wrong?" he asked when she stiffened.

She sat up partway, taking the afghan with her and leaving his upper half exposed. The sadness in her eyes worried him. After the miserable two weeks they'd endured, he never wanted to see her upset again. He still couldn't believe she'd forgiven him and was willing to give him another chance. He'd do everything in his power to avoid disappointing her again.

"Putting the Rh factor aspect aside, what if I'm never able to carry a baby to term?"

He grabbed her hand and kissed the palm. "I love you, Lanelle."

She opened her mouth to speak, but he rushed on. "If we're blessed with children, they'd be a complement to our relationship, not the center. We can try to have kids if you want, or look into other options when the time is right. Or we could grow old with just the two of us hanging around in ratty jogging suits together."

She smacked his shoulder. "I wasn't expecting company."

He flinched and rubbed the offended area, smiling. "What do you say? Will you have me as your one and only man? Or do you want to just have incredible sex every chance we get?"

"How about both?"

"We can make it happen." Throwing the blanket off, he lifted her. "Now show me to your bed."

She fanned herself with the hand not wrapped around the back of his neck. "I do like a strong, macho man who takes charge."

His step faltered. "Since when?"

"That's right, I don't." Her eyes held a teasing glint. "You'd do well to remember that, Mr. Sanderson."

He snickered. "As if you'd ever let me forget."

"Up the stairs. It's the first door on the left. And…"

"Yes?" He looked into her eyes. She had to be the most gorgeous woman in the world.

"I love you, too."

Hastening his steps, he resolved to make sure she always knew how much he cherished her.

Chapter 30

Dante's hands displayed a slight tremor when he took the keys to lock Lanelle's door. After dating for the past seven months, Lanelle knew him well enough to recognize that something was off. He had yet to compliment her on the red satin halter-top dress, which exposed shoulders he liked to kiss without warning. She'd bought it with him in mind.

"Do you mind if we go to The Cervante for dinner?"

A strange request, considering he'd never mentioned eating there before, maybe because she knew it more as one of the most elegant hotels in the city rather than a restaurant. "Not at all." Just as long as they could be together.

His cool and slightly clammy hand grasped hers. She touched her free hand to his forehead and felt no excess of heat. "Are you okay? We could cancel and stay home if you aren't feeling well."

The rapid shake of his head told her he was hiding something. "I'm fine. It's just been a long day."

Within thirty minutes, Dante handed his keys to the valet. The car ride had been a little unsettling, with Dante rambling on about everything from work and his family to the political candidates from the party he supported for the state election. Not his usual style.

Once inside, he led her in the opposite direction of the hotel's restaurant.

"Where are we going?"

"You'll see."

They stopped in one of the many spectacular ballrooms where she'd attended galas and dinners in the past. His eyes shone in the dim lighting of the hallway.

Lanelle stared at him, attempting to figure out what was going on.

The room glowed with an iridescent light as he opened the door and led them in. Other than the gleaming marble floor, high-hanging crystal chandeliers and elegant shimmering curtains she wouldn't mind turning into a formal gown, the room stood empty. Lanelle paused as she waited for him to explain.

"This is one of my favorite floors." His hushed tone kept her still. "I worked on it myself, from choosing the slabs to helping with installation."

"It's beautiful."

"It's original Carrara marble. I flew with it on the flight from Italy ten years ago."

Dante moved closer and laid his hands on her hips. "You're standing on a piece of Italy." Reaching for her fingers, he walked her farther into the room. Lanelle remained silent and followed. He stopped, pulled something from his jacket pocket, turned and went down on one knee.

Covering her mouth failed to stifle her gasp when he opened the small box. Her gaze roved from the ring in Dante's hand to his earnest eyes.

"Eliana Lanelle Gill Astacio Murphy," he said with a shaky voice, "when I first met you, I was awed by the intense effect you had on me. I searched for you, only to have you find me. Destiny brought us together, not once but three times."

Tears blurred her vision.

"The two weeks we spent apart after our trip to Italy were the worst of my life. But we endured the misery and my stubbornness and came together stronger than ever. You are my world, Lanelle. My everything. I once again vow to make your dreams come true by giving you the children you desire. Your happiness is my main concern."

Lanelle felt sure her heart would burst at any moment. She loved this man so much.

"Nothing will ever get in the way of our love again. I promise I'll be a good husband and father to our children. Will you marry me?"

She laid a hand on her lower abdomen. Was she ready to enter into the world of matrimony again? This time with a man she couldn't help loving, even when she'd tried to avoid it. He belonged to her, just as she belonged to him. She went down on her knees and looked up into his beautiful eyes, no longer afraid to tell him what she'd known to be true for the past couple of days. "I hope you won't mind being a father sooner rather than later."

It took him a moment to comprehend her words. "Are you pregnant?"

She nodded, still unable to read anything but shock in his expression. "Only six weeks, but the doctor confirmed it yesterday. I didn't know how to tell you."

His whoop of joy ricocheted off the walls of the empty room. Springing up, Dante wound his arms around her, lifted her off her feet and swung her around. She held on, willing the world to stop so they could experience this bliss forever.

Panting, he lowered her, steadying her when she wobbled. "I love you so much, Lanelle." Then he knelt again and spoke to her belly. "I love you, too. You have a wonderful mother waiting to cherish you, so make sure to grow strong and come out healthy to meet her." He nuzzled his face against her abdomen.

When he stood again, he had tears in his eyes. "You never answered my question. Will you marry me?"

How could she doubt what she'd say? "Of course I will."

He hugged her tight, then released her to look into her eyes. "You have made me the happiest man in the world. This is for you." He took the ring out of the box, reached for her left hand and placed it on her finger before kissing her with a gentleness that added more tears to her eyes.

When he ended the kiss with one sweet, soft peck on her forehead, Lanelle whispered, "If there were more powerful words to express how I feel about you, Dante Leroy Sanderson, I'd use them. I love you." She looked down at her flat belly. "My dear child, you have a father who will do anything in his power to make sure you always know you are loved." She chuckled. "I won't let him spoil you too much, though. Do your ultimate best to come out and meet the best man your mother has ever known."

She wound her arms around his neck and kissed him in a way she was sure would leave no doubt in his mind as to how much she treasured him and the gift he'd bestowed.

When Lanelle ended the kiss, she stared at the solitaire emerald-cut diamond. "It's stunning. It looks like the same ring I chose when I played the 'if money were no object' game with Vanessa on the shopping excursion in Rome."

"It's the very same one. My niece is a cunning rascal. I think she knew long before either of us that we'd end up together."

"And you remembered?"

"How could I not? Vanessa took a picture of it and sent it to my phone, saying, and I quote, 'This is the ring you're to buy for Lanelle when you propose. Don't mess it up.'"

Lanelle burst out laughing as she caressed his face. "And you didn't. It's perfect."

"Just like our lives together will be."

* * * * *